DICKINSON AREA PUBLIC LIBRARY

W9-CRD-990   4

F Fraser, Anthea D2498 V. 06
Fraser, Anthea.
Six proud walkers

(David Webb novel #6)

WITHDRAWN

SIX PROUD
WALKERS

SIX PROUD
WALKERS

ANTHEA FRASER

A Crime Club Book
Doubleday
NEW YORK LONDON TORONTO SYDNEY AUCKLAND

DICKINSON PUBLIC LIBRARY

All of the characters in this book are fictitious,
and any resemblance to actual persons, living or
dead, is purely coincidental.

A Crime Club Book
Published by Doubleday, a division of
Bantam Doubleday Dell Publishing Group, Inc.
666 Fifth Avenue, New York, New York 10103

Doubleday and the portrayal of a man
with a gun are trademarks of
Doubleday, a division of Bantam Doubleday Dell
Publishing Group, Inc.

Library of Congress Cataloging-in-Publication Data
Fraser, Anthea.
Six proud walkers / Anthea Fraser.
p.   cm.
"A Crime Club book."
I. Title.
PR6056.R286S59 1989
823'.914—dc19   88-21924
                                                        CIP
ISBN 0-385-24615-3
Copyright © 1988 by Anthea Fraser
All Rights Reserved
Printed in the United States of America
February 1989
First Edition
OG

76884

For my brother and sister-in-law,
Christopher and Mary Roby,
in their Silver Wedding Year.

THE WALKER FAMILY

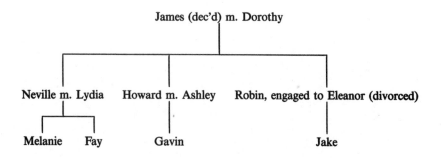

James (dec'd) m. Dorothy

Neville m. Lydia   Howard m. Ashley   Robin, engaged to Eleanor (divorced)

Melanie   Fay   Gavin   Jake

GREEN GROW THE RUSHES-O

I'll sing you one-o!
(Chorus) Green grow the rushes-o!
   What is your one-o?
One is one and all alone and evermore shall be so.

I'll sing you two-o!
(Chorus) Green grow the rushes-o!
   What are your two-o?
Two, two, the lily-white Boys, clothéd all in green-o,
(Chorus) One is one and all alone and evermore shall be so.

I'll sing you three-o!
(Chorus) Green grow the rushes-o!
   What are your three-o?
Three, three the Rivals,
(Chorus) Two, two, the lily-white Boys, clothéd all in
  green-o,
One is one and all alone and evermore shall be so.

I'll sing you four-o!
(Chorus) Green grow the rushes-o!
   What are your four-o?
Four for the Gospel-makers,
(Chorus) Three, three the Rivals,
Two, two, the lily-white Boys, clothéd all in green-o,
One is one and all alone and evermore shall be so.

I'll sing you five-o!
(Chorus) Green grow the rushes-o!
   What are your five-o?
Five for the Symbols at your door, and
(Chorus) Four for the Gospel-makers,
Three, three the Rivals,
Two, two, the lily-white Boys, clothéd all in green-o,
One is one and all alone and evermore shall be so.

I'll sing you six-o!
(Chorus) Green grow the rushes-o!
    What are your six-o?
Six for the six proud Walkers,
(Chorus) Five for the Symbols at your door, and
Four for the Gospel-makers,
Three, three the Rivals,
Two, two, the lily-white Boys, clothéd all in green-o,
One is one and all alone and evermore shall be so.

I'll sing you seven-o!
(Chorus) Green grow the rushes-o!
    What are your seven-o?
Seven for the seven Stars in the sky, and
(Chorus) Six for the six proud Walkers,
Five for the Symbols at your door, and
Four for the Gospel-makers,
Three, three the Rivals,
Two, two, the lily-white Boys, clothéd all in green-o,
One is one and all alone and evermore shall be so.

I'll sing you eight-o!
(Chorus) Green grow the rushes-o!
    What are your eight-o?
Eight for the April Rainers,
(Chorus) Seven for the seven Stars in the sky, and
Six for the six proud Walkers,
Five for the Symbols at your door, and
Four for the Gospel-makers,
Three, three the Rivals,
Two, two, the lily-white Boys, clothéd all in green-o,
One is one and all alone and evermore shall be so.

I'll sing you nine-o!
(Chorus) Green grow the rushes-o!
    What are your nine-o?
Nine for the nine bright Shiners,
(Chorus) Eight for the April Rainers,

Seven for the seven Stars in the sky, and
Six for the six proud Walkers,
Five for the Symbols at your door, and
Four for the Gospel-makers,
Three, three the Rivals,
Two, two, the lily-white Boys, clothéd all in green-o,
One is one and all alone and evermore shall be so.

I'll sing you ten-o!
(Chorus) Green grow the rushes-o!
    What are your ten-o?
Ten for the ten Commandments,
(Chorus) Nine for the nine bright Shiners,
Eight for the April Rainers,
Seven for the seven Stars in the sky, and
Six for the six proud Walkers,
Five for the Symbols at your door, and
Four for the Gospel-makers,
Three, three the Rivals,
Two, two, the lily-white Boys, clothéd all in green-o,
One is one and all alone and evermore shall be so.

I'll sing you eleven-o!
(Chorus) Green grow the rushes-o!
    What are your eleven-o?
Eleven for the Eleven that went up to heaven, and
(Chorus) Ten for the ten Commandments,
Nine for the nine bright Shiners,
Eight for the April Rainers,
Seven for the seven Stars in the sky, and
Six for the six proud Walkers,
Five for the Symbols at your door, and
Four for the Gospel-makers,
Three, three the Rivals,
Two, two, the lily-white Boys, clothéd all in green-o,
One is one and all alone and evermore shall be so.

I'll sing you twelve-o!
(Chorus) Green grow the rushes-o!
   What are your twelve-o?
Twelve for the twelve Apostles,
(Chorus) Eleven for the Eleven that went up to heaven, and
Ten for the ten Commandments,
Nine for the nine bright Shiners,
Eight for the April Rainers,
Seven for the seven Stars in the sky, and
Six for the six proud Walkers,
Five for the Symbols at your door, and
Four for the Gospel-makers,
Three, three the Rivals,
Two, two, the lily-white Boys, clothéd all in green-o,
One is one and all alone and evermore shall be so.

                                        "Traditional"

SIX PROUD
WALKERS

CHAPTER 1

The July sky was a molten blue, and the sun scorched his back through his thin shirt. Leaning over the newly restored battlement of the twelfth-century tower, Chief Inspector Webb looked down on a high-walled garden and saw—murder. Quite literally saw it spelt out in flowers, the letters formed of vivid red blooms against a background of gold.

He turned to Hannah, who was gazing across the village to the woods and fields that encompassed it.

"Take a look down here," he said quietly.

"Where?" Her bare brown arm brushed against his, her hair swung forward as she followed his pointing finger.

"My goodness!" she said. "Someone has a macabre sense of humour."

"If that's what it is."

She turned to look at him. "Oh, come on, David! You're off duty; stop thinking like a policeman!"

For a moment longer he stared down, the accusing red letters branding themselves on his retina. Then he took her arm and moved her round the tower. "No point in drawing attention to it," he said. "Isn't that the place we're going to this afternoon?"

"Yes, the Old Rectory; where the fête's being held."

"Not much sign of activity."

"It'll be the other side of the house."

The sound of approaching voices echoed up the spiral staircase, and some people about to descend waited for the newcomers to emerge. When both groups had dispersed, Webb said, "Didn't you say you know the people?"

"That's right, the Walker family. The younger daughter's at Ashbourne."

"Are they given to accusations of murder?"

"I doubt it. They're the Walkers of Walker & Fairfax. You know—Broadshire Porcelain. They won the Queen's Award for Export again this year. But if you're curious, ask Mr. Walker yourself. He's the church warden on duty."

"I shan't bother, but given the chance, I'll inspect those flowers more closely." He looked down at the honey-coloured houses and the ford which gave the village its name, now dried to a mere trickle in the heat wave. All the gardens were ablaze with colour, a tumbling mass of roses, hollyhocks, delphiniums, and marguerites. But as far as he could see, none of the rest of them spelt "murder."

"It's a pretty little place you've found yourself," he commented.

Hannah sighed contentedly, turning and leaning her back against the warm stone. "Yes, aren't I lucky? And Paula actually thinks I'm doing her a favour."

"Well, you are. Not everyone would be prepared to move in and look after three highly eccentric cats for a month."

"I shall love every minute of it. I'll spend my time sunbathing and having cool drinks. After a fraught term, what could be more relaxing?"

"Talking of cool drinks, how about sampling one of the pubs for lunch?"

"Good idea. There's one near the cottage which looks promising. Would you like to lead the way down?"

After the sunlit open air, they were temporarily blinded by the plunge into semi-darkness, and the dank walls of the staircase struck chill on their hands. The stone steps were worn into hollows by centuries of climbing feet, and the voices of people still up on the parapet reached them like echoes from another world. The ringing chamber, with its narrow windows, offered a brief respite before the final descent to the cool, flower-perfumed church. Over by the font, a man was being interrogated by an elderly woman in a big hat.

"That's the Mr. Walker I know," Hannah said quietly, "Fay's father."

"It's still run as a family firm, then?"

"Yes, by three brothers, I believe, and their mother."

The elderly woman moved away, and turning, the church warden caught sight of Hannah. He came across with a smile.

"Miss James—welcome to Honeyford! Miss Welling told us you'd be cat-minding while she's away."

Hannah took the hand he offered. "Good morning, Mr. Walker. May I introduce David Webb?" The two men shook hands.

"We've been admiring your restoration work," Webb said. His glance, deceptively casual, took in every detail of the man in front of him. Mid-forties, average height, light brown hair, pleasant, confident manner. Managing Director or somesuch, no doubt.

"Yes, marvellous to know it's finished at last. We've been fund-raising for over two years." Walker smiled ruefully. "Though no doubt there'll soon be something else to raise money for—the penalties of inheriting ancient buildings. I hope you're both coming to the fête?"

"Oh, certainly."

"Good. The vicar's opening it at two." He glanced at his watch, then nodded towards the staircase. "Are there many still up there? Once they're all down, I can go home for lunch."

"I don't think they'll be long. We'll see you later, then."

The churchyard lay baking in the midday peace, its forgotten tombstones leaning drowsily towards the parched grass. There was the hum of small insects, a bird calling in one of the high trees. At the gate, a faded board informed them they'd been visiting the Parish Church of St. Clement.

" 'Oranges and Lemons,' " said Webb predictably. They walked down the sloping path towards the gateway of the Old Rectory.

"Where does the vicar live, if not here?"

"Over there." Hannah nodded to a much smaller house immediately opposite. "The days when the clergy lived in huge houses are long gone."

Webb paused, looking up the driveway to the Old Rectory. It was a handsome, three-storeyed house, in the pale grey stone which contrasted here and there with Cotswold gold. On the right of the drive, a vast lawn spread green and lush—obviously the result of careful watering over the past few weeks. A succession of stalls edged it on three sides, at which figures could be seen busily setting out their wares. At the far end loomed the large, white outline of a marquee. Webb glanced to the left of the drive, but a laurel hedge blocked off what lay behind it.

The group whom they'd left up the tower were now approaching, and Hannah could see Mr. Walker locking the church door. "Come on," she urged, "we don't want him to catch us peering up his drive."

They moved on down the path, between the drystone garden walls over which a profusion of plants spilled in extravagant largess.

"I wonder how the place got its name," Webb mused. "The 'ford' bit's obvious, but 'Honey' could refer equally to beekeeping at some time, or to the colour of the stone."

"Sorry, but it's neither. It was originally Huna's Ford, according to the guidebooks."

"Who the hell was he?"

"Some Saxon lord, no doubt."

Webb grinned. "Trust a schoolmarm to know that. I prefer my own explanations."

They had reached a fork in the path. The main stem continued down to the High Street, while the right-hand branch led to the cottage where Hannah was staying.

"The pub I mentioned is just round the corner," Hannah said, as they passed her gate. One of the cats lay spread out on the path, eyes blissfully closed. Another sat watching them unblinkingly from the gable over the front door. Then they were past and, rounding a bend in the road, found themselves facing a charming old pub nestling under a roof of mossy stone, with ancient oak beams supporting its framework. Opposite it, on a triangle of grass, grew an enormous chestnut tree with a wooden seat round its trunk, and here, in the shade, a group of lunchtime drinkers chatted animatedly. Webb felt it would have been more in keeping had they been gap-toothed ancients in smocks rather than young people in designer jeans, but even Huna's Ford moved with the times. He followed Hannah into the welcome cool of the inn.

"Is that you, Neville?" Lydia Walker came hurrying out of the drawing-room. "Thank goodness you're back. The men have some question about the marquee. Would you go and have a word with them?"

Her husband kissed her cheek. "Couldn't Robin have seen to it?"

"He had a look, but as you know, he's not exactly practical."

Neville smiled. "All right. Pour me a G and T, and I'll see what I can do."

He walked through the cool elegance of the drawing-room and out of its open French windows, where the merciless heat awaited him, seeming to shrivel his skin with its dragon's breath. Mad dogs and Englishmen, he thought humourously.

They'd made good progress since he left to go on duty. The stalls were all up, many of them decked with gaily coloured bunting, and the worthy ladies of the parish were engaged in setting out piles of knitted garments, cakes, toys, books, and records. A coconut shy had been erected, and a hoop-la stall. For how many hundreds of years had such innocent amusements been partaken of in rural England?

Neville felt a sense of permanence and well-being, which banished for the moment worries about the factory and the Francombe order. After all, it was the weekend, and one that promised to be enjoyable, since after the fête, they were giving a birthday party for his nephew. Neville always enjoyed family gatherings. Though he envied Howard his son, women these days were as able managers as men. His mother more than proved that, and his daughters, he felt sure, would follow the family tradition.

How lucky he was, he thought, pausing to congratulate one of the stallholders on her display. He had so much—health, wealth, success, this beautiful home, and a thriving business. Above all, he had the family. He felt a surge of love for them all—for Mother and Lydia and the girls, for Howard and Ashley and Gavin, for Robin—even, he thought wryly, for Eleanor. Mother had reservations about her, but after all, Robin was nearly forty. It was more than time he settled down, and if Eleanor was what he wanted, so be it.

Reaching the marquee, Neville ducked his head and went inside to sort out the problem.

"Glad to see you're supporting home industries, Miss James!" Neville nodded smilingly at the jars of home-made jam and pickles in Hannah's basket. "Enjoying yourselves?"

"Very much," Webb answered. "You've a magnificent garden. Do you work in it yourself?"

"Not often, to be honest. Too many other calls on my time. Fortunately, we inherited gardeners when we moved here ten years ago—a father and son. They keep it well in trim."

They'd be unlikely, though, to sow flowery accusations of murder. "But no doubt some of your family garden?"

If Walker was surprised by his persistence, he was too polite to show it. "My elder daughter does. She showed interest very early on, and we gave her her own patch to look after. It paid dividends: she's taking a course at Broadminster Horticultural College."

"Would her patch by any chance be over by the wall near the church?"

"How on earth d'you know that?"

"We saw it from the tower, but we'd like a closer look, if it's not inconvenient. It's—fairly striking."

"Well, good for Melanie. I'll come with you; I haven't been down there lately, and I shouldn't be needed till they draw for the raffle."

Leaving the crowded lawn behind them, they crossed the wide gravel drive and went through a gap in the laurel hedge. But even then their view was limited. To create interest, the available space had been divided into a succession of small areas, each hidden from the next by trellises and hedges. The result was a series of miniature gardens, each with its own characteristic: a profusion of roses in one, a small pool in another, a rockery filled with alpine plants. Finally, bypassing the last hedge, they came upon the high boundary wall, beyond which rose the church with its newly restored tower. Between them and the wall lay the bed which interested them, the deep, burning gold proving to be French marigolds and, carved out in their midst, the vivid scarlet of salvias.

Hannah wished suddenly that they hadn't come. What would poor, pleasant Mr. Walker make of that garish display?

"I presume it's a pattern of some sort?"

Neither of them answered him. In silence they walked round to the front of the bed till they were facing the flowers and their bizarre message. Neville Walker gazed at it unbelievingly, and Hannah saw the colour leave his face.

"My God!" he said, barely audibly. Then, with a strained laugh, "Well, it adds a new meaning to saying it with flowers."

"Have you any idea what it refers to?" Webb asked.

"*Refers* to? Good lord, man, it doesn't *refer* to anything. How could it? It's just a—sick joke. I shall have a word with that young lady." He looked up at the tower, closed to the public this afternoon. "Heaven knows how many people have seen it from up there."

"Perhaps it was work she was set at college," Hannah suggested. "There must be quite an art in forming letters."

"But she didn't sow the seeds. Those flowers were raised in

the greenhouse, and only planted out in April. I remember now, Jack mentioned Melanie'd asked for some." He paused and repeated, almost to himself, "April."

"Even if it was set work, it was an odd word to choose," Webb said mildly. "Anyway, we thought it worth mentioning."

"Indeed yes, I'm very grateful. I'll get Jack to dig it up on Monday."

Dorothy Walker drew her favourite chair to her bedroom window and sat down. From here, she'd a grandstand view of the lawn and the throngs of people milling about.

She wished she didn't feel so ill. Four more days, and she'd know, one way or the other. Suppose she really did have that frightful disease? She'd never even *heard* of it till three weeks ago, when Bruce suggested this latest set of tests. Should they prove positive, what appalled her even more than the inevitable advance of paralysis was the fact that the disease was hereditary. Which meant she'd have to tell the boys. She couldn't leave them to find out after her death, as they were bound to.

She pulled herself to her feet, leaning on the windowsill for support. Neville was walking back across the drive with a man and woman. She wondered where they'd been. The woman looked familiar; wasn't she the deputy head of Fay's school? That's right, someone had said she was staying at Wychwood.

A queue seemed to be forming down to her left, and, seeing the cause of it, Dorothy clucked her tongue with annoyance. Eleanor signing autographs. How utterly ridiculous. Why should merely reading the news on television warrant such attention? She did so wish Robin had chosen differently. There was the boy too, and although he seemed a nice child, it was an added responsibility.

Her attention was brought back to the scene below. A disturbance had broken out near the Bran Tub—some jostling, and raised voices. Heads were already turning in that direction. Dorothy narrowed her eyes, trying to identify the source of the trouble. A shock of red hair, suddenly flailing fists: oh dear, it was the Ridley boy. She'd have to go and sort things out.

Wearily, she turned and hurried from the room. By the time she reached the scene, Ridley was being restrained by Neville and Howard. He was obviously drunk and ready for a fight. "Here comes the Queen Bee in person!" he jeered, catching sight of her. "Queen Bee of Honeyford! Good, that!"

Aware of the interested crowd, Dorothy said quietly, "I suggest you go home, Mr. Ridley. You're clearly unwell."

"Aren't you going to turn my pockets out first? I might have nicked something from the stalls. Like father, like son, they say." His face distorted suddenly and he began to weep. Distressed, Dorothy turned away as his wife, red-faced with embarrassment, came to claim him.

"I'm that sorry, Mrs. Walker," she murmured with bent head. "He's still upset, see—he didn't mean no harm."

"Harm?" Ridley raised his ravaged face, and Dorothy took a step back from the hatred in his eyes. "I've not started yet, duck. These bloody Walkers killed my dad, and I'll make 'em pay for it—every last one of 'em!"

"Come on, Dick," his wife urged desperately, tugging at his arm. "Let's go home and have a nice cup of tea." And to everyone's relief, he allowed himself to be led away.

Webb and Hannah, on the fringe of the crowd, watched them go. "I wonder what that was all about," Webb said. "I must say, it's been a more interesting afternoon than I'd expected, one way or another."

"Oh, Miss James, there you are!" Lydia Walker had appeared beside them. Her flushed cheeks were the only indication that she'd witnessed the scene just over. "I was hoping to have a word with you; I'd meant to call round and welcome you to the village, but what with one thing and another, I haven't got round to it."

Hannah murmured some reply, and introduced Webb. The church warden's wife, it seemed. He wondered if she'd seen her daughter's flower-garden. She was a lovely woman, tall, slim, immaculately groomed, her smooth black hair coiled low on her neck. But, interestingly, he was aware of underlying disquiet. The explanation could lie in the unpleasantness of a moment ago; on the other hand, it might be more deep-seated.

He pulled himself up. After a lifetime of assessing people, it was difficult to switch off on social occasions. Hannah was right: he was off-duty, and Mrs. Walker's inner tensions were no concern of his.

He let his attention wander, turning to watch a group of teenagers who were trying, amid much laughter, to dislodge a row of coconuts. Behind them, also watching their endeavours, was a woman in her late thirties. She was wearing narrow white linen trousers and an emerald green shirt. Her pale brown hair hung straight and smooth, curving in towards the line of her jaw, and as he watched, she hooked a stray strand of it behind one ear. Something about her stance, casual yet assured, almost arrogant, arrested his attention, and, perhaps sensing his scrutiny, she turned and met his eyes. Hers were a cool sea-green, their expression faintly questioning. For a long moment they looked at each other, neither of their expressions changing. Then, to Webb's consternation, she began to walk towards him.

Had she read something into that held gaze? He fought down the urge to walk quickly in the opposite direction. But Lydia had also seen her approach, and Webb realized with a mixture of feelings that it was she who was the newcomer's objective.

"Ashley, come and meet Miss James, Fay's deputy headmistress. And Mr. . . . Webb, was it? My sister-in-law, Ashley Walker."

Her hand was long, slim, and cool, its grip firm. She said to Lydia, "What was all that commotion just now?"

"Oh—nothing, really. Just someone who'd had too much to drink."

"I saw Howard and Neville being masterful."

There was a brief, uncomfortable pause. Then Lydia said, "Miss James is looking after Paula's cats while she's away."

"Oh yes?" Clearly the strangers were of no interest, and Webb, aware that she knew he'd been watching her, sensed a deliberate rebuff. But even as he registered it, the cool eyes turned to him. "Are you staying at Wychwood too, Mr. Webb?"

"No," he answered levelly, ignoring the implication. "I've just been helping Miss James move in."

Halfway through his reply, he'd lost her attention. Damn her! he thought, and was surprised at his vehemence. She said to her sister-in-law, "If anyone wants me, I've gone home. See you later," and started to move away. Then paused, looking back over her shoulder. "Nice to have met you." The cliché was presumably for them both, but she was looking at Webb. Then she was swallowed up in the crowd.

Lydia said, "Ashley's son is eighteen today. We're giving a party for him this evening."

"They live nearby, then?" Webb thought he spoke casually, but he felt Hannah's glance.

"Yes, just outside the village."

A voice over the Tannoy announced that the raffle draw was about to take place, and people began to converge on the table set up for the purpose. Lydia excused herself and moved away. Webb said, "Do you want to stay for this?"

Hannah shook her head. "I never win raffles."

"Then how about a cuppa in the peace of Wychwood garden?"

"You're on."

Moving against the tide, they walked down the gravel driveway to the gate.

"You realize something?" Webb said, threading Hannah's arm through his. "Something we should have realized before?"

"What's that?"

"I can't spend the night at the cottage."

"Oh, David! It—"

"Really. You heard that thinly veiled question. These people know you professionally, and if they discover you entertain men friends overnight, it will do neither you nor the school any good. I'll book in at a pub. There must be one that's residential."

"But you were going to come every weekend I'm here."

"I still can. By some quirk in the moral code, no one'll blink an eyelid if we spend the days and evenings together."

Hannah sighed. "You're right, of course. I have to be above suspicion."

"Exactly. Imagine if the girls got to hear of goings-on."

"Perish the thought. Right—we'll abide by the rules, and what we do *before* nightfall is strictly our own affair."

"I couldn't have put it better myself," Webb said.

CHAPTER 2

Lydia stood on the terrace, wondering whether she should again ask the group to turn down their amplifiers. The music seemed very loud, and she didn't want to offend the neighbours, though, as Neville had pointed out, all their close neighbours were here.

The party seemed to be going well. The afternoon's stalls had been dismantled, and the marquee, which had served earlier as the tea tent, was now the setting for a more sumptuous feast. Damask, silver, and crystal were already in evidence and the caterers, neat in their uniforms, were beginning to set out the food.

Neville came up behind her and slipped an arm round her waist. "All right, darling?"

"So far, so good. Did you speak to Melanie?"

"I did. She was quite unrepentant."

"She wouldn't have expected anyone but the family to see it."

"That's no excuse. It could have resurrected the whole thing again. Thank heaven Mother didn't stumble on it."

"It was probably done on the spur of the moment, to give vent to her feelings."

"She'd vented them quite enough already. Anyway, I'll get Jack to dig the bed over on Monday. Lord knows what Miss James and her friend made of it." He ran a finger round the inside of his collar. "I said it would be too hot for dinner jackets."

Lydia patted his arm. "Never mind, darling, you look very smart."

Neville shaded his eyes to look across the sunlit grass. "I see Clive's dancing with Fay again," he said. Melanie was also watching her sister with some anxiety. Though Fay had said little, Melanie suspected she was still keen on Clive, and the feeling seemed mutual. He was holding her closely, his face pressed against her hair, and was whispering into her ear. Across the garden, Melanie heard Fay's light laugh.

She really wasn't enjoying this evening a bit, what with Daddy blowing his top about the flowers, and now this. The Tenbys shouldn't have been invited; there'd been an understandable coolness since the Clive and Fay business, but Mother, bless her heart, was bending over backwards to smooth things over. Darkly, Melanie wondered if that was a mistake.

The scene from the terrace, Dorothy thought, was almost Edwardian, the women and girls in long dresses and the older men in dinner jackets. She approved of the formal wear; it made the evening more of an occasion.

Soon, now, it would be supper-time, and afterwards, the present-opening ceremony. She felt a touch of apprehension, patting the reticule in which her cheque lay waiting. She hoped Gavin would understand, but she really couldn't bear it if he were to disappear for a whole year, drifting aimlessly about the Continent. And, she thought with a rush of cold fear, she mightn't be here when he returned.

She pulled the cobwebby lace more closely round her shoulders and smiled determinedly up at the vicar, who was bending to speak to her.

Eleanor Darby sipped her Pimms, her eyes on her son. He was sitting on the grass, clasping his knees and watching the dancers gyrating to the music. Poor Jake; this social gathering really wasn't his scene. He was a quiet child, who'd rather spend his time painting than in physical activity. With luck, his interest in art would form a link with his future step-father; they were

Robin's designs which decorated the famous Broadshire Porcelain, his sketches which evolved into the figurines sought after as collectors' pieces.

Jake had made little comment on the proposed marriage. Eleanor gathered he wasn't in favour, but was prepared to make the best of it. And Robin was very good with him; it wasn't every man who'd take on a ten-year-old stepson.

She recalled the surprise of her friends on learning her plans. True, her first marriage hadn't been a success, and in the six years since the divorce she'd been aware of becoming more independent and less tolerant, with only herself to please. *Was* she doing the right thing, marrying Robin? Was he, in marrying her? The family weren't overjoyed, that much was obvious.

The family! Everything came back to that. A happy family, goodness knows, is one of life's blessings, but this one seemed *too* close, immersed in its own affairs and resentful of intruders. And surely that was stultifying; for what hope had the younger ones, growing up in an enclosed, self-sufficient world of successful men and beautiful women, of finding partners as interesting or attractive as their own family?

This evening was a case in point. She said to Robin, "It's a bit hard on Gavin, being saddled with us at his party."

He looked surprised. "An eighteenth birthday's a milestone —of course he wants us here. And there are at least two dozen of his friends as well."

"Most of whom are also lumbered with their parents."

"Well, they're friends of Neville and Lydia." He smiled at her. "Come on, admit it! You're miffed because we don't fit in with all your media jargon about generation gaps."

"I just know I wouldn't have had the vicar at *my* eighteenth."

"Relax—George is OK."

Eleanor made a grimace. "Except he regards me as a scarlet woman."

"Now you're being ridiculous."

She shook her head. "Not only am I from the Big Bad City, but I'm divorced as well, so the youngest scion of the family can't be married in church. Bad news!"

"He probably doesn't approve of me either, but I don't lose any sleep over it."

"Well, we'll be away from his black looks in London, thank God. Village life and its mores would drive me demented."

Robin was silent. This was a point he'd avoided discussing, and he wasn't going to embark on it now. He was quite prepared to spend the first months of their marriage in London, working from Eleanor's flat and delivering his artwork as necessary. In fact, the breathing space would be welcome, since in his absence he would evolve in everyone's mind into a married man. But it could only be a temporary arrangement. Before long, they'd move back to Broadshire, if not to Honeyford itself. Eleanor might protest, but he was confident of being able to win her round.

Gavin Walker, though unaware of his prospective aunt's sympathy, would not have welcomed it. He was enjoying being the guest of honour, and in any case, life was good. A-levels were behind him, and ahead stretched the enticing prospect of a year abroad, to which he'd been looking forward for the past two years.

"Just think of it," he said dreamily into his partner's ear, "strolling down the Champs-Élysées and eating in Left Bank cafés. Then taking a train to Italy on the spur of the moment—Florence, Venice, Rome. It'll be magic, Debby, sheer magic!"

"You're determined to go, then?" Debby sounded less enthusiastic.

"Of course I am. I've been dreaming of it for years, and Grandma's cheque will put the seal on it."

"I thought she wasn't keen on you going?"

"She'd rather I went straight to Oxford, but that's only so I'd join the firm a bit sooner. Good grief, I'll be there the rest of my life! One year at this stage won't make any difference."

"It will to me," Debby said in a small voice, and he gave her a squeeze.

"But if I didn't go abroad, I'd be at Oxford. And I'll send you postcards. Boy!" he exulted, "I can hardly believe it! A whole *year*, all to myself, to do exactly what I want, *when* I want. It's the best birthday present anyone could have!"

The supper was as elegant and delicious as the guests confidently expected. Cones of smoked salmon stuffed with cream cheese nestled pinkly between glistening black caviar and the pale green of asparagus, while white-coated servers stood behind joints of beef, chicken, and ham, carvers poised. Heaped bowls of salad concealed melon and strawberries among their more conventional leaves, and cups of cold soup were accompanied by garlic-flavoured croutons and chive-speckled sour cream.

It was dusk now, and small tables had been set up, each with its flickering candle in a protective glass container. Coloured fairy-lights glowed in the trees, and floodlights illuminated the facade of the house. The trio who had provided music for dancing now played a selection of musical-comedy numbers, awaking nostalgia in the older guests.

"You have to hand it to the Walkers," Pamela Tenby remarked sotto voce to her husband, "they know how to put on a show."

"Then you're glad pride didn't prevent you coming?"

She smiled. "I suppose so. Anyway, Clive was so set on it."

"He seems to have picked up the threads again." Derek Tenby nodded towards his son, now sitting on the grass with Fay and tucking into his supper. "Perhaps there's been a change of heart."

"I'd still like to know what it was all about. When I tackled Lydia at the time, she became all flustered and I couldn't get any sense out of her. Granted, diplomatic relations have been resumed, but I'll never forgive them for hurting Clive like that."

"Oh, forget it, love. It's not worth worrying about, specially if it's blown over now."

But Derek Tenby's assumption was misplaced. Fay's father was at that moment arranging for the two to be separated.

"I'm rather concerned about Fay, Richard," he was saying to the vicar's son. "She's been a bit off-colour recently. Could I ask you to keep an eye on her, see she doesn't catch cold and so on?"

Richard Mallow wasn't deceived; he'd been wondering how far Clive's licence would extend. He was unsure of the background, but Fay was a friend of his sister's and he wouldn't like to see her hurt.

"Of course, sir. Don't worry, I'll look after her." And as Neville watched, he walked over to where she still sat with Clive and, bending down, raised her to her feet. Neville couldn't catch what he said, but, with an apologetic little murmur to Clive, she obediently moved away with him.

Danger averted, thought Neville with relief, then brought himself up with a smile. Danger? Hardly an appropriate word in the circumstances. But for some reason he felt ill at ease this evening. The unpleasantnesses of the afternoon, those lurid flowers followed by the scene with Ridley, had unsettled him more than he cared to admit. In particular, Ridley's drunken threats had lodged in his mind. *These bloody Walkers killed my dad, and I'll make 'em pay for it—every last one of 'em!*

Neville realized he was standing exactly where Ridley had stood when he made those threats. Irrepressibly he shuddered, and moved away to find his wife.

Supper over, everyone made their way to the drawing-room for the present-opening. It began with a brief speech from Howard, in which he thanked Neville and Lydia for the party and proposed his son's health. Then, sipping their champagne, everyone sat round benignly while Gavin opened one parcel after another from friends and friends' parents. Wallets, compact discs, cufflinks, after-shave piled up on the table beside him till the room resembled a gift department. And all the while, Dorothy sat tightly upright on her chair, fingers grasping her velvet reticule. Only when, after profuse if embarrassed thanks all round, Gavin turned to the family offerings, did she open it, withdraw the envelope, and, leaning forward, place it on top of the pile of parcels.

Gavin smiled across at her. "I think I know what that is, Gran, so I'll save it till last."

O God, she thought in panic, let it be all right. Let him understand. As the ritual continued, that white oblong with its scrawled black writing remained unnervingly on the edge of her vision. Whatever had they bought each other before all these electronic marvels? she wondered, eyeing the personal computer, the Sony Walkman, the miniature portable television. And now only the gifts from his parents and herself remained, both of which were concealed in envelopes. Howard and Ashley's contained a set of car keys, and Gavin jumped up in delight to hug them.

"The car's waiting at home," Howard said. "I didn't want you driving back after all this champagne."

Gavin plied his parents with excited questions about the make and model. "I'll be able to take it abroad with me," he ended with satisfaction. "Getting about'll be much easier with my own transport. Which," he flashed a smile at Dorothy, "brings me to Grandma's present. And if this is what I hope it is—"

His impatient fingers tore at the paper and the envelope fell to the floor as he unfolded the cheque inside it. Smiling in anticipation, the rest of them waited for the last, exuberant expression of thanks. But Gavin's own smile had faded. He stood staring as though in shock at the piece of paper in his hands. Then he raised his eyes and met his grandmother's.

"I don't understand," he said numbly.

"It's clear enough." Belated misgivings made Dorothy's voice crisper than she intended. "It comes, of course, with my best love. And it will be trebled if you give up that hare-brained idea of travelling, and go to Oxford in October."

Everyone seemed frozen into an embarrassed tableau. Gavin said hoarsely, "You mean you're holding a gun to my head?"

"My dearest boy, nothing so dramatic. But as I think you know—"

"Let me get this quite straight," he interrupted. "You're saying that unless I do what you want, this is all you're prepared to give me. Is that right?"

Howard moved forward protestingly. "Gavin—"

Dorothy moistened her lips. "Quite right. But is it so much to ask? After all, once you're established in the firm, you'll travel as a matter of course, and in a great deal more comfort. It's not—"

"But I want to go *now!* It'll never be the same again!"

"Gavin, I'm sorry. I hoped—"

"You're not sorry at all!" he broke in harshly. "You're very pleased with yourself, because you think you've won. But you're wrong, Grandmother. I'm not going to give in to blackmail. And this"—he began to tear up the cheque into minute pieces while everyone watched him, mesmerized—"is what I think of your birthday present! And of you!" and as the tatters of paper drifted to the floor, he strode across the room and out through the French windows.

CHAPTER 3

The back garden at Wychwood was small and entirely enclosed by a high stone wall. Up, down and along this grew, climbed, tumbled and leaned a host of sweet-scented plants, great swathes of roses, jasmine, honeysuckle and clematis, and in the beds beneath it, stocks, nicotiana and phlox added their own perfume to the warm, heady air.

Webb and Hannah sat in the deepening dusk on the small patio, drinking their after-dinner coffee and idly listening to the music which drifted down the lane from the Old Rectory. The black cat, Oswald, had leapt uninvited on to Webb's knee and was proceeding to wash itself thoroughly. Arthur the tabby had set off soft-footed to check his territory, and Pirate, he of the black eye-patch, lay in the open doorway immediately behind them.

Webb stretched comfortably. "Rural bliss," he said. "How can anyone choose to live in a town?"

Hannah topped up his coffee cup. "Never mind; you've got four more weekends to look forward to."

He smiled. "Just as well the pub's reasonable." He'd booked into an old inn on the High Street, on the corner where Hannah's lane joined the main road.

"I'm sorry about that. You could have stayed here if I hadn't advertised your presence by dragging you to the fête."

"Oh, I wouldn't have missed it for anything. How the other half lives." He thought briefly of Ashley Walker.

"With murder in their flower-beds? I wonder if Mr. Walker was serious about digging it up. I'll try to sneak a look on Tuesday."

"Tuesday?"

"When I go for coffee."

"I didn't know you'd been invited."

"Yes, this afternoon. Your attention was wandering at that point."

"Can you blame me? All that feminine chitchat." But he was grateful for the concealing dusk. "Anyway," he added, "there's another reason why I'd rather stay on here. I'm not looking forward to next week."

"Why not?"

"Because a woman DI's being foisted on us, and what's more she's being put in my office."

"But why? I thought your complement was complete?"

"Crombie's course has been extended, and his replacement's still off ill. He had a perforated ulcer and, as if that wasn't enough, picked up an infection in hospital, poor bloke. So if a major incident blew up, we'd be undermanned."

"Then it's just the fact that she's a woman you object to? Really, David, how chauvinistic!"

"No, it's because she's coming to Shillingham 'for family reasons.' Which means she's probably hoping for a permanent appointment."

"What's wrong with that?"

"I don't want her permanently in my office, that's what's wrong, and God knows where else there's room for her." He lifted the cat and deposited it gently on the paving stones. "In the meantime, I'd better be getting down to the Horse and Groom. It's after eleven, and I don't want to find myself locked out."

As Webb reached the corner of the High Street, a car skidded out of a turning further up the road and scorched past him. He'd a brief impression of three people inside. Probably coming from the Old Rectory and probably tight, he thought grimly. He stood looking after its tail lights as they dwindled rapidly in the distance. Then, with a shrug, he went into the pub.

Inside the car, Howard Walker remarked mildly, "No need to break any speed records, darling."

"Don't criticize my driving," Ashley said tightly, "or you can get out and walk."

"I can't think why you insisted on driving."

"Because I want to get home before dawn."

Gavin said sulkily from the back seat, "She can't wait to tear me off a strip."

"And don't think you don't deserve it," his father retorted. "You behaved appallingly, and in front of everyone, what's more. God knows what our friends thought."

"I object to blackmail, even when it's wrapped up in large cheques." He gripped the sides of his seat as his mother slewed the car through the gateway of their home and drew up at the door in a hail of flying gravel.

Howard said, "I wasn't happy myself at the thought of you swanning round Europe for a year. Lord knows what kind of company you'd have got into."

"I see you're using the past tense. Does that mean you think she's won?"

Ashley slid out of the car, leaving the door open. Her husband leant across to close and lock it.

"Gavin, don't let's have another scene. It's your birthday, damn it. I don't want to play the heavy father."

"But you don't mind her playing the heavy grandmother. It's so grossly *unfair!*"

Howard felt a twinge of sympathy. That last sentence was the child's age-old protest against adult supremacy. In silence they followed Ashley into the house. She had flung herself down on the sitting-room sofa and kicked off her shoes.

"I think we could do with a nightcap," Howard said.

As he poured the drinks, he searched for a way round the situation. Better if he tried to defuse it; Ashley wasn't in the mood to be tactful, and Gavin would lash out at the first hint of criticism. He handed them each a glass, looking from one frowning, well-loved faced to the other. Then he sat down with his own drink and cleared his throat.

"Now, Gavin. Try to see your grandmother's point of view, there's a good chap. You're the only boy in your generation—it's natural she should want you in the firm as soon as possible. As it is, there'll be a three-year gap while you're at university, but at least you'll be doing vacation work in the factory and learning the ropes. Whereas if you go waltzing off for a whole year, you might well lose the taste for work altogether—opt out of Oxford and everything else."

"Ah! That's the whole point, isn't it? She's terrified once I'm away from family influence, I might decide not to go into the beastly firm at all."

Howard's heart missed a beat, but he answered levelly, "She's too much faith in your good sense to think that."

"How much faith has she in Melanie's and Fay's? They'll probably get married, most girls do. Suppose their husbands have their own interests and don't want them spending all their time at the factory?"

"We're not concerning ourselves at the moment with Melanie and Fay. Look, Gavin, your grandmother's not *forbidding* you to take a year off."

"She'd better not try!"

"All she's done is give you a cheque for your birthday and promise to treble it if you'll go straight to Oxford."

"And since that cheque is only a third of what she gave Melanie, I'm being penalized unless I give in to her. Which, as I said, is blackmail." He sounded perilously close to tears. "Damn it, Dad, I've been looking forward to that year. All through A-levels I was thinking, Once this is over, I'll be free! And I was counting on that cheque to start me off. Now, thanks to that bloody-minded old woman, the whole thing is in the air. I wish I'd rammed her miserable cheque down her silly old throat!" And, clattering his glass down on the table, he stumbled to his feet and hurriedly left the room.

Howard took off his spectacles and polished them on his handkerchief. His face looked oddly naked without them. "I'm afraid that wasn't a very useful exercise," he said.

Ashley swung her feet to the floor. "Let him sleep on it. He may see sense in the morning. Mind you, he has a point. He's entitled to the same amount as Melanie, but he only gets it if he does what he's told."

"He's her favourite grandchild, you know," Howard said quietly. "And she's getting old. I've noticed a big change in her the last month or two. She hasn't the same 'go' and she sags if she thinks no one's looking. I'd say the root of it is that she doesn't want to part with him for a whole year."

"She could have been open about it, instead of trying to force his hand like this."

"But she was. Didn't he tell you? Ever since she learned what he was planning, she's been trying to talk him out of it. But he's as stubborn as she is, and he wouldn't budge. That's why he resents it so much now."

"What worries me is that he may have got her back up, after the way he behaved this evening."

Howard smiled tiredly. "She's hardly likely to cut him out of her will, if that's what you're thinking. That would defeat her own object, wouldn't it?"

"I suppose so." She stood up abruptly. "God, I'm tired. It's been a long day." He rose too and came over to her, cupping her cool, bare elbows in his hands.

"Try not to worry, darling." Her eyes were on a level with his. In them he read a brief flare of hope, followed by dispirited resignation. He let his hands drop and she turned away.

"I love you," he said. She nodded and left the room.

It was only as he was preparing for bed that Howard realized Gavin hadn't asked to see the car. He sighed. Perhaps things would right themselves in the morning.

Eleanor stretched her lithe, cat-like body and took the lighted cigarette Robin handed her. To her amusement, she'd been allocated a room in the main house rather than in Robin's top-floor flat. Once all the bedroom doors were closed, he had come to join her.

"What did you make of that scene this evening?" she asked idly.

Robin bent and kissed her throat. "Gavin's always had a temper. When he was small he used to throw tantrums, but it's some time since I've seen him let fly as he did this evening."

"In his place, I'd have let fly too."

"It's Mother's money; she can apportion it how she likes."

"Oh, come on, Robin! She was using it as a lever, and you know it. The fact that Melanie's eighteenth was only last year makes it all the more pointed. I'm not surprised Gavin told her what she could do with it."

He leant back his head and exhaled a stream of smoke. She lay watching him, the long line of his throat, the hollow at the base of it, the strength of his chest and shoulders.

"You don't like it when I criticize your beloved family, do you, even though I'll soon be part of it? Look, love, this has to be said. There's something claustrophobic about you all, and it worries me sometimes. You're a closed circle—'Trespassers keep out.' But some day, someone's going to break away. I hoped you might be the first, but it looks as though it'll be Gavin."

"He's not going to 'break away,' Eleanor. There's no reason why he should. Mother wasn't putting any pressure on him."

"Not much, she wasn't. She puts pressure on all of you, though you don't seem to realize it. For instance, why are you marrying me?" She held up a hand as he began to speak. "OK, you love me, I accept that. But you've loved other women, and you didn't marry them. Why me? Getting married wasn't my idea, and I suspect it wasn't yours, either. But your mother thought it time you settled down and did your bit about providing an heir. She's not wild about your choice, but at least I've proved I'm not barren."

"Eleanor!"

"OK, love, it's probably the booze talking, but let me finish. She may think she owns the lot of you, body and soul, but she doesn't. Just because you and Neville and Howard were good little boys and did what Mummy told you, it doesn't mean the next generation will."

"You talk as if we were forced to join the business. We weren't. It never occurred to any of us to do anything else. Damn it, the firm's been going for two hundred years, passing from father to son all along the line. Of course it must continue. Surely you see that."

"Dear Octopus," she said.

An hour later, back in his own bed, her question about their marriage was still in his head. It was true Mother wanted another grandson, but he'd more pressing reasons for his decision, reasons which made a change of status not only desirable but imperative. Once and for all, he must extricate himself from a very messy situation, and this was the only way to do it. Then perhaps those terrible memories would stop haunting him.

And she was right about his not liking her criticizing the family. Dear Octopus, she'd called it. But she'd settle down once they were married, and all would be well. Things always came right in the end. Turning on his side, Robin drifted into sleep.

On the floor below, Dorothy Walker lay waiting for the trembling to cease. It had not been a happy day. First the Ridley boy at the fête, then Gavin, which was so much worse. Oh, *why* had she acted so stupidly? Her illness was clouding her judgment. Because she'd no time to let events take their course, she'd tried to force the issue. With disastrous results. The *things* that boy had said! Surely he didn't mean them?

She pressed a hand to her jumping heart. She'd not intended to blackmail him—of course she hadn't. It was a loathsome idea. In fact, as soon as she'd reached her room, she'd written another cheque for the full amount. When she felt calmer, she'd send for him and hand it over. Apologize. Oh God, let it be all right. Let *everything* be all right.

It was Sunday afternoon, and Nina Petrie reached up on tiptoe to slide the last suitcase on top of the wardrobe. There—that was better. She stood back and surveyed the room, with its flowered wallpaper and heavy blue curtains, its narrow single bed and the stain on the rug. She'd spilt a bottle of nail varnish on it at the age of sixteen. She smiled faintly, remembering, which was a luxury she didn't often allow herself. Looking back made the good things seem better and the bad worse than they'd actually been. Better to live in the present.

But moving home was unavoidably a time of stock-taking. She wasn't the same person who once owned this room, who'd lain in that bed the night before her wedding, too excited to sleep. She was ten years older and, she hoped, correspondingly wiser.

During those ten years, she'd acquired a much-loved daughter, built up a steady career in the police force and her husband had become an ex-husband. And now that Mum's health wasn't so good, she'd arranged for her promotion move to be to Shillingham so they could all live together.

It was to her advantage as much as Mum's; there would be someone at home when Alice came in from school or when she herself was called out at night, which was increasingly likely. And on the career side, it would be exhilarating to work in the busy county town instead of the quieter ambience of Oxbury. She'd been warned, though, that her present position was temporary; Inspector Crombie was on a prolonged course at Bramshill, and initially she'd be sitting in for him. However, if she proved useful at Divisional Headquarters, the Chief Super had hinted that a niche would be found for her. Nina was quietly confident that it would be.

Alice's voice sounded from below. "Mummy! Gran said to tell you tea's ready!"

"Coming!" With a last, satisfied look about her, Nina ran downstairs.

Back at his desk, Webb's thoughts turned more than once to the flowery accusation at the Old Rectory. It probably meant nothing, but he'd have liked to know the reason for it. Furthermore, such musings invariably led to Ashley Walker, which annoyed him. He hadn't particularly liked her, but nor could he banish the memory of her poise, her careless acceptance of the impact she made. She was the type of woman, he told himself, who drove a fast sports car and had an impossibly low handicap at golf. Those traits did not appeal to him; he'd never cared for aggressive women. Notwithstanding, she had lodged in his mind, and he resented the intrusion.

He also resented Nina Petrie, he acknowledged, gazing moodily at her bent head. Not that she'd put a foot wrong so far. She was keeping herself to herself, but her presence altered the entire atmosphere of the office, and it no longer seemed his own.

Oxbury appeared to think well of her. "Alert, efficient, innovative" were words he remembered. He looked her over assessingly. She was of small build—no Junoesque Ashley Walker here—and her hair was of the frizzy, naturally curly variety, almost black. Eyes unexpectedly blue under straight black brows, and a pleasant smile, he recalled, which lit up a rather stern face. Not that she'd smiled often. To be fair, he'd given her nothing to smile about.

For the rest, her bust was on the heavy side, though her waist was trim and she'd good legs. He could see them now under the desk, ankles neatly crossed.

Hannah's words suddenly came back to him, and he shifted uncomfortably, admitting that he wouldn't have catalogued a male colleague's attributes like that. It was a police officer who sat over there, he reminded himself, and he'd make sure he treated her as one, regardless of gender.

Though apparently intent on her work, Nina was aware both

of his scrutiny and his disapproval. She'd done her best, she reflected sadly, but he didn't like her. It was a pity, but it needn't rule out a perfectly workable relationship. On one thing, however, she was determined. She wasn't going to play the admiring little woman to his macho policeman. They were both here because they were able, quick-thinking, and, in varying degrees, well thought of. He might not like her, but she'd earn his respect. On that, she was determined.

She shut him out of her thoughts and went on with her report.

On the Tuesday, it rained. Hannah heard it as soon as she woke, drumming on the rafters just above her head. Oswald, who had resisted all her blandishments to come inside the previous night, had apparently sought shelter through her window and now lay curled on the dressing stool.

She slipped out of bed and went to the window. It had been raining for some time. The gutters which, during dry spell, had become clogged with blown petals and twigs, were miniature torrents along which the debris swirled helplessly towards the waiting grids. At the gate, the cherry tree stood bowed under its weight of drenched foliage.

Hannah went down to shower in the minute bathroom of which Paula was so proud. The other two cats greeted her as she emerged, winding themselves round her legs, running ahead of her up the steep staircase, then stopping halfway, so that she almost tripped over them. They strolled nonchalantly into the bedroom and, with one accord, jumped on the sleeping Oswald and edged him off the stool. There was a brief boxing session, after which all three sat down and washed themselves. Hannah wasn't sure what points had been scored or by whom, but honour was apparently satisfied.

The rustling sound of rain filled the room, soft and soothing. There could be no surreptitious peep at the flower-bed in this weather. Flanked by her escort, she went down for breakfast.

* * *

The coffee party was held in the conservatory, which led off the dining-room at the back of the house. Comfortable, deeply cushioned chairs were positioned overlooking a part of the garden Hannah hadn't seen before. Immediately below was a wide, paved area with a swimming pool in its centre. Today, rain made pock-marks on the surface of the water.

"How lovely to have your own pool!" she exclaimed. "It's always been an ambition of mine."

"Then please make use of it while you're here," Lydia Walker told her and, at her instinctive protest, "Really—I mean it. There are days when no one goes near it, and it seems hardly worth the maintenance. You'd be doing us a favour."

"Well, if you're sure, I'd love to." Hannah took the chair indicated and settled back as coffee was brought in.

It was a moment or two before she became aware that no one was quite at ease. Perhaps it was her own presence which was inhibiting, though they'd greeted her with friendliness. Only gradually did she identify the undercurrent as embarrassment, and Ashley Walker as its centre. Hannah was curious. Obviously these women knew each other well. Why, suddenly, should there be constraint between them?

She realized with a start that Lydia was addressing her. "More coffee, Miss James?"

She held out her cup with a smile. "I'd feel much more comfortable if you'd use my first name. It's Hannah."

There was a relieved murmur of assent. At least, she thought, I've done my bit to ease the tension. She added, "How did the party go? We were sitting outside, and heard the music."

Immediately she'd spoken, she knew she'd pinpointed their discomfort. Damn! Everyone's eyes dropped and Lydia flushed.

"I hope it didn't disturb you," she said.

"Not at all; we enjoyed it."

It was Ashley who answered her question. "It went extremely well, thank you. A great success."

Two of the other women started to speak at once and broke
off with embarrassed laughs. Hannah thought, Something happened at the party, and they were all there. What could it have
been?

After a stumbling start, conversation resumed and Hannah,
feeling it wise to revert to being an onlooker, studied one after
another of those present.

Beside the two Walker women, there were three others. Inez
Pratt, introduced as the doctor's wife, was a strong-featured
woman with dark hair wound round her head in braids. She
wore no makeup and was dressed in a black T-shirt and full
cotton skirt. Her legs were strong, brown and hairy, her bare
feet thrust into leather thonged sandals. On an ethnic kick,
Hannah decided.

Barbara Mallow had arrived at the same time as herself,
crossing the road from the vicarage. She was pale and fair-
haired, with a determinedly pleasant expression. Hannah suspected she might find it harder than her husband to love her
neighbours, and wondered where the Walkers featured in her
popularity chart.

Lastly, there was Pamela Tenby, who, catching Hannah's
glance, closed one eye in a wink. Hannah smiled back, guessing
her summing-up had not gone unnoticed. Mrs Tenby was au-
burn-haired and pale-skinned, with oversized spectacles
perched on her nose. She seemed to be observing the proceed-
ings with slightly malicious amusement. Hannah hoped there'd
be the chance of a private word with her.

They were on the point of leaving when Dorothy Walker
came into the conservatory. And it was only then that Ashley
betrayed a hint of nervousness.

"Please don't let me disturb you," the older woman said as
they started to rise. "I'm just on my way out. Ashley dear,
would you ask Gavin to come to tea with me tomorrow? About
four o'clock; I've an appointment earlier, but shall be back by
then."

"Yes—yes, of course."

Dorothy nodded, smiled on them all, and went out again. Hannah had only seen her from a distance on Saturday and was struck now by her air of frailty, the skin stretched tightly over her cheekbones.

At her side, Pamela Tenby said, "I'll run you back."

"Oh, it's not far."

"Far enough in this weather." And to underline her words, thunder growled in the distance. They moved in a bunch through the dining-room, formal in mahogany, to the wide, panelled hall. Hannah wondered if erstwhile clerics had enjoyed that magnificent woodwork, or whether later owners, more blessed in worldly riches, had installed it.

"Don't forget about the pool," Lydia reminded her as they said good-bye. "No need to phone—come whenever you like."

Pamela's car was the little red mini in the drive. "And what," she asked, as they emerged onto the road, "did you make of all that?"

"How do you mean?"

Pamela laughed. "You can't fool me. You got us all sussed out, didn't you?"

"I hope it wasn't as obvious as that. I was just a little intrigued by the—atmosphere."

"I'm not surprised. The reason for it was an almighty row between Gavin and his grandmother at the party, though it looks as though a truce is in the offing."

"What was it about?"

"Money, my dear. Filthy lucre. His birthday cheque wasn't as big as he'd expected."

"It seems a little ungracious."

"Well, there's more to it than that. But it was highly embarrassing, and Lydia must have been wishing she hadn't arranged the coffee morning."

"I suppose you know the family well?"

"Well enough."

"But you're not a close friend?"

"No. To be honest, a little of the Walkers goes a long way.

They're obsessed with family pride—the line going back God knows how long, and all that jazz. They've not much time for lesser mortals."

"You sound rather bitter," Hannah said quietly.

"Sorry. It's just that my son was going out with young Fay for a while. Quite keen on her, and she seemed to reciprocate. Then all of a sudden, attitudes changed and it was made pretty clear his attentions were no longer welcome."

"You mean Fay changed her mind?"

"Nothing so simple. The family changed theirs. With no explanation. Clive was very upset at the time."

"Was he at the party?"

"Oh yes; basic civilities have been maintained."

They had drawn up outside Wychwood. Hannah said, "You were talking about the unbroken Walker line, but the firm's Walker & Fairfax. What happened to them?"

"Dorothy was the last of them—an only child. And since James Walker's brother and two cousins were killed early in the war. They were more or less forced together, to prolong the dynasty." She gave the last word a veneer of sarcasm, then, slightly ashamed of herself, added, "Still, however politic, there's no denying it was a love-match, right up to his death."

"I see. Well, thanks for the lift. Would you like to come in for a minute?"

"No, thanks; Clive'll be waiting for his lunch. Nice to have met you, Hannah."

The little car drove off in a spray of water. Hannah stood for a moment, lifting her face to the rain. It felt warm and earthy, pattering on her skin. Different from town rain somehow. Pushing the gate open, she walked up the path. She might not have seen the flower-bed, but she felt she'd learned quite a lot about the Walkers.

CHAPTER 4

Nick Carstairs dropped his racquet on the grass and joined
Melanie at the iron table. Yesterday's rain had passed and the
sun shone again.

"We'll have a return match when there's a court free—OK?"

She stretched out her long legs, sipping her lemonade. "If
you like."

"Such enthusiasm!" He glanced at her astutely. "Family row
blown over?"

"Which one?"

He raised his eyebrows. "You don't do things by halves, you
Walkers. How many have you had?"

"Two to my knowledge, but I suppose you mean Gavin."

"Right. I thought your grandmother'd have a stroke or
something when he lashed out at her like that."

"Gavin has a quick temper," Melanie said slowly, "but it
was Grandma's fault for handing the cheque over in public."

"But it was the specified time, surely?"

"All the same, she must have known how he'd react. It was
almost as though she was challenging him."

"Does that mean you're on Gavin's side?"

"It's not a question of *sides*, Nick. But if I had to back one of
them, it would be Gavin, yes."

"Insurrection in the camp, no less."

"My grandmother," Melanie said intently, "is a ruthless old
woman. She'll go to any lengths to get her way, and it doesn't
matter who gets hurt in the process."

Nick looked at her in surprise. "Hey, isn't that a bit strong?
She seems such a gentle old lady."

"That's because you're not family. There's a different set of rules for us; we have to conform."

"Would the other row by any chance be between you and her?"

"No, me and my father."

"Well, well. And I thought you were such a devoted family. Is it serious?"

"He was furious at the time, but it's over now."

Nick smiled crookedly. "And you're not going to tell me any more about it."

"Correct."

"All this time I've envied you your large and supportive family, but perhaps I'm lucky there's just Mum, Dad, and me."

"No," she said slowly, "I wouldn't swop them really. They're OK." She looked up at him from under her thick, straight brows. "Forget what I said about Grandma. I shouldn't have. She wants what she thinks is best for us."

"And the business," suggested Nick shrewdly.

"There's nothing wrong with that. It's our livelihood, after all."

Nick drained his glass. "I was surprised to see Clive there. Is it on again with Fay?"

"No." As though aware that her answer was abrupt, she added, "You know what it's like in the village. If we hadn't invited the Tenbys, there'd have been a lot of raised eyebrows."

"But how *is* Fay? She looks very pale and dreamy these days."

"She's all right." This time there was no disguising the sharpness in her voice.

"I was only asking," Nick protested mildly.

"And I was only answering." Melanie pushed her chair back, coming to her feet. "Look, those people are coming off Court 3. If you want another game, we'd better go and nab it."

For a moment he looked up at her, at the determined line of her jaw, the thick, tawny hair hanging straight almost to her shoulders, the windblown fringe. A strong character, his Melanie. And however much she criticized her family, it was clear no one else may.

With a shrug he bent to pick up his racquet and followed her down the grass slope to the court.

It was closing time, and, with bad grace, Dick Ridley allowed himself to be escorted out of the Swan and collapsed onto the bench outside. He should have been at work, but after a night's heavy drinking he'd not been able to face it. He'd phoned in and reported sick—said he'd a bad head, which, Lord knew, was the truth, though Cath wasn't pleased.

"You'll be fired, Dick, if you take any more time off, and there are plenty of others to snap up your job."

It was to escape her nagging that he'd left the house, hoping the hair of the dog might help. It hadn't, though. He was still churned up about the Walkers and the way they'd seen him off the premises on Saturday. Thought no end of themselves, the lot of them, but they owed him something. If it hadn't been for them, Dad would still be alive. The least they could do was make some kind of recompense.

The glare from the pavements was hurting his eyes and he closed them, leaning his head against the warm stone wall behind him. Bloody Walkers, he thought with drowsy belligerance. He'd show 'em, take the superior smiles off their faces. Plotting befuddled revenge, his head fell forward and he slept.

Clive Tenby, lying on his back in a field outside the village, was also thinking of Saturday. He'd believed he could bluff it out, seeing Fay again, but he'd been wrong. It still hurt. She'd seemed glad to see him too. Only her rotten family was keeping them apart. It was Mr. Walker who'd sent Richard over—Clive had seen them talking. But *why*, for heaven's sake? It wasn't as if he wanted to *marry* her. Dash it all, he was only eighteen. In the beginning, her parents had seemed in favour of their seeing each other—even encouraged them. Why, suddenly, around

Easter, had they changed their minds? They wouldn't even let him see her, to ask what was wrong.

He rolled over onto his stomach, pulling out a blade of grass and carefully extracting the sweet, juicy inside. Fay never went to the tennis club any more, nor the disco or the coffee bar. She seemed to spend all her time with that drip Rachel Mallow. For weeks he'd hoped he'd run into her somewhere, find out what'd happened, but he never had.

He sat up abruptly, beating his fist on the ground as a decision crystallized. He'd go and confront them, demand to know what they had against him. If it was due to a misunderstanding, perhaps it could be straightened out and all would be well again. What's more, he'd go now, before he got cold feet.

He ran to the hedge where he'd left his bicycle and wheeled it through the gap on to the main road. Then, before he could change his mind, he turned it in the direction of Honeyford.

Feeling conspicuous, Hannah walked up the drive of the Old Rectory, her towel under her arm. Changing facilities hadn't been mentioned, and she was wearing her swimsuit under her dress.

Without the stalls and marquee, the lawn looked even larger, spreading its smooth greenness over to a thick clump of trees by the far wall. Keeping close to the house, Hannah walked the length of the terrace and rounded the corner. Ahead of her, the paving ended at the glass wall of the conservatory and below it, set amid its sunny flagstones, the pool invitingly awaited her.

She hesitated, shielding her eyes and looking up at the windows. There was no sign of life. She hoped Lydia had informed the others of the invitation she'd extended. Pushing aside her doubts, Hannah slipped off her dress and dived into the water.

Those blasted flowers were still bothering him. Not only their cryptic message, but the effect it had had on Walker. Webb was convinced he'd known what it meant. Why else should the colour have left his face like that?

He ran a hand through his hair, then reached for the internal phone. "Ken, come in for a minute, will you."

Nina Petrie looked up, but he didn't glance in her direction. If he wanted her to leave the room, she thought, he could ask her.

"Yes, Guv?" The little, sandy-haired sergeant had a quick smile for her.

Webb leant back in his chair. "I'm not going barmy, am I? There *haven't* been any suspicious deaths in Honeyford over the last six months?"

"Honeyford? Not that I recall, Guv. I'll check if you like."

"No, don't bother; I know damn well there haven't. There was just an outside chance something might have been passed off as natural causes."

"You mean an overdose or something?"

"I mean murder," said Webb, and at that, Nina's head came up again.

Jackson looked startled. "You reckon someone might have slipped something over on us?"

Webb shook his head irritably. "Forget it. It was just a hunch," he said.

Outside the Swan in Honeyford, Dick Ridley slowly awoke and rubbed his stiff neck. His sleep had done him little good; his mouth was dry, his head still ached, and the Walkers still filled his thoughts. He lurched to his feet, gazing blearily up the High Street. Why not go up there now? The men would be at the factory, and the old woman, too, but Mrs. Neville should be in. She might be a softer touch than her husband—see his point of view. Worth a try anyway. He turned and started to walk unsteadily in the direction of the Old Rectory.

The taxi drew up and the driver reached behind him to open the door for her. Steadying herself with one hand, Dorothy climbed down and fumbled for her purse. She was having to concentrate on even the most mundane of actions, and it took her several minutes to calculate the amount of the fare plus the tip she wished to give the driver. She, whose brain used to work like a computer.

"Sure you're all right, ma'am?"

She met the kindly eyes and smiled. "Yes. Yes, thank you. Quite all right."

Moving slowly, she went up the steps to the front door and opened it with her key, pushing up the catch as she did so, so that Gavin could come in without ringing. Behind her, she heard the taxi turn on the gravel and drive away.

The grandfather clock chimed the half-hour, making her jump. Three-thirty. Time to compose herself before he arrived. In the drawing-room, the tea-trolley was laid ready, covered by a cloth. She'd forgotten, when she asked to see Gavin, that it was Phyllis's afternoon off. Not that it mattered. She hoped she was still capable of boiling a kettle.

It was hot in the room and she opened the French windows, drawing the curtains a little way across to keep out the sun.

God help her, she thought suddenly, clutching at the arm of a chair as her legs went weak; she'd have to tell the boys. How would they take it?

Don't think about it! With the strength of will that had stood her in such good stead over the years, she pulled herself upright, clamping her mind down on the painful half-hour with her consultant. Like Scarlett O'Hara, she'd think of it tomorrow, when she'd had time to recharge her batteries.

A sound from the hall made her turn sharply. Gavin was early. Never mind, it would be over all the sooner. Marshalling her resources, she faced the doorway, awaiting her grandson.

The strangled, gasping scream was loud enough to jolt Hannah from her sunbaked doze. She sat up quickly, heart pounding. Had she dreamt it? Even as the thought formed, a voice cried hysterically, "Help! Oh my God, somebody help me!"

Barefoot, Hannah raced along the terrace and hurtled round the corner of the house. Outside the open French windows,

Ashley Walker was leaning over the low terrace wall, sobbing and retching.

"What is it? Whatever's wrong?"

Ashley turned a wild face towards her, showing no surprise at her presence. "It's Mother. She's on the floor in there—dead!"

Hannah gazed at her in horror, then turned towards the windows. She heard Ashley say, "No—don't—" and, dodging her outstretched hand, parted the half-drawn curtains and stepped inside.

It was the smell she noticed first: the warm, sickly, unmistakable smell of blood. Then she saw Mrs. Walker crumpled on the floor, her face—her face—

Hannah swayed, feeling the bile rush into her mouth. God, don't let her faint. David—

Shudderingly she pulled herself together, shivering in her still-damp swimsuit. Because the face wasn't a face any longer, simply a red, pulpy mess, out of which protruded white pieces of bone. And the blood—blood was everywhere, glinting in pools on the carpet, caking the dead woman's clothes, splashed on the chair above her body. On the hearth, its grisly business done, lay a discarded poker.

Hannah stumbled back outside. "The phone—" Her voice was a croak. She cleared her throat and tried again. "Where's the phone?"

"In the hall." Ashley spoke jerkily, between gasps. "Don't go back that way—the front door's open."

Hannah hesitated. "Will you be all right for a minute, while I call the police?"

Ashley nodded and she set off along the terrace, grateful for its warmth on her bare feet. The front door opened to her push. The telephone, immediately visible on an oak settle, took on the aspect of a lifeline, a link with the sane, outside world. Luckily she knew the number.

A woman's voice sounded in her ear, blessedly calm and matter-of-fact. "Shillingham CID."

"Chief Inspector Webb, please. It's urgent."

"I'm sorry, madam, he's not available at the moment. Can I take a message?"

Hannah said, "But he *must* be!" Then, more rationally, "I'm sorry. Someone has just been murdered. Mrs. Dorothy Walker, of the Old Rectory, Honeyford."

"Honeyford?" Nina interrupted.

"Yes. I'm speaking from there now. Can somebody come at once?"

"Of course." The relevant information was quickly obtained. "You're quite sure she's dead, Miss James?"

"Quite sure." Hannah's voice shook.

"Then please stay where you are and don't touch anything. I'll get on to the local police-station. They'll be there within minutes, and we won't be far behind them."

"And Mr. Webb?"

"He'll be contacted as soon as possible."

By the time the local bobby arrived on his bike, Hannah had regained a modicum of composure. Ashley'd accompanied her back to the pool and waited while she slipped on dress and sandals. Hannah understood how she felt. They were united by the unspeakable horror they'd seen, and for the moment they needed each other's presence.

PC Hobson, unused to violence in his peaceful village, was as shocked as they were. Mrs. Walker was—had been—an important member of the community, and he was stunned by her brutal end. Having satisfied himself, at some cost, that there was no chance she was still alive, he had taken up a position outside the French windows, "preserving the scene," as he told them. Ashley's request to phone her husband had been stalled. "Best wait till CID get here, ma'am. They'll know what should be done."

Side by side on the low wall, the two women awaited the next influx of police.

*   *   *

It was some minutes before Webb could extricate himself from the court, where he'd been giving evidence, and make his way to a phone in response to his bleeper.

Jackson answered, excitement in his voice. "Got second sight, have you, Guv?"

"Look, Ken, if you're wasting my time—"

"That murder in Honeyford you were asking about. It's happened. A Mrs. Walker, at the Old Rectory."

Webb felt his chest constrict. "*Which* Mrs. Walker?"

"Dorothy's the name. Inspector Petrie's gone straight there, with Harry Sage."

"Who reported it?"

"A Miss James. Would that be the young lady you—"

"Wait for me outside. I'm on my way." Dropping the phone on its hook, Webb strode out of the Courthouse.

Webb and Jackson were escorted along the terrace by PC Hobson and stood surveying the scene from the French windows.

"It's all right, Constable," Webb said drily, seeing the man's anxiety lest they inadvertently destroy evidence. "We can see all we need without going inside. Has the police surgeon been called?"

"Yes, sir, but Dr. Pratt's already been, seeing as how he's local and knows the deceased. He didn't move nothing. Didn't need to; it was clear she was dead."

"Quite." Webb stood for some minutes noting details and drawing sketches in his pocket-book. The savagery of the scene sickened him, and he was appalled to think that Hannah'd been subjected to it. As he turned away, Dr. Pringle and the Scenes of Crime team were coming along the terrace.

"It's all yours," Webb said shortly. "Not a pretty one. I'll be in the house if you want me."

Hannah was giving her statement at the hall table. She broke off as he came in, rising to her feet as though pulled by strings. It took all her self-control not to run to him. Harry Sage, turning to see what had distracted her, also rose.

"This is Miss James, sir, who reported the incident."

"Murder," Hannah corrected in a clear voice. "Don't let's mince words, Sergeant; it's murder."

Webb said gently, "I gather you found her?"

"No, Ashley did. I'd been swimming in the pool. It must have happened while I was there." Only as she spoke did she realize the significance. Suppose the murderer'd looked out of a window and seen her? It would have been a simple matter to hold her head under water—

"Hannah." Webb raised his voice, noting Sage's surprise at the Christian name. "It's all right. I'll speak to you later." He turned to Sage. "Where's Inspector Petrie?"

The man jerked his head in the direction of the dining-room. "In there, sir. With Mrs. Walker. That is—"

"I know who you mean, Harry." He went down the hall with Jackson behind him, and opened the dining-room door. Ashley was sitting on one of the mahogany chairs, hugging herself as though for warmth, her face pale and streaked with tears. The contrast to the confident, self-assured woman he'd last seen added to the poignancy. As a result, Webb spoke more brusquely than he'd intended.

"Thank you, Inspector. I'll take over now."

Nina flushed. "I'm half-way through the statement, sir."

"I said I'll take over."

"Very well." She stood up, shuffling her papers together.

Ashley was looking at him in bewilderment. "What are you doing here?"

"Have the next of kin been informed?" he asked Nina.

"A call was put through to the factory." Her voice was clipped. "No details—just an urgent request to come at once. Mr. Neville Walker's away and not expected back till tomorrow. They've no way of reaching him."

"Very well. Let me know when the rest of them arrive, and field their questions till I get there."

She nodded and left the room, head high.

"Exactly what do you think you're doing?" Ashley demanded ringingly. "Who *are* you?"

"Chief Inspector Webb, Shillingham CID."

For a moment she stared at him. Then she said softly, "You bastard."

Jackson blinked. There were undercurrents here he didn't understand. Poor Mrs. Petrie'd had her head bitten off, and now it seemed the Governor knew this woman. Was that why he'd asked about murder? Jackson decided a low profile would be politic and seated himself at the carving table, out of her sight and at an angle to Webb.

"You never said you were in the police," Ashley accused.

"There was no reason to. Mrs. Walker, I'm very sorry about your mother-in-law. How did you come to find her?"

She closed her eyes briefly. "I've just been through that with—"

"Tell me. Please. Why did you call here this afternoon?"

"Well, because Gavin—" She broke off, looking up at Webb with widening eyes. He waited in silence. After a moment, taking a grip on herself, she continued. "My son had been invited to tea. I was on my way home and decided to drop in and join them."

"Was he here?"

"Obviously not."

"He'd been and gone?"

"No!"

"You can't be sure of that, Mrs. Walker."

"He wasn't due till four. It was only just after when I arrived."

"He might have come early."

Ashley shook her head decidedly. "Mother'd said she had an appointment earlier, and not to come till four."

"What kind of appointment?"

"She didn't say."

"Would she have driven herself to it?"

"I've no idea."

"This is your sister-in-law's house; where is she?"

"She has French Conversation on Wednesdays."

"And where were you yourself this afternoon?"

An eyebrow lifted, but she answered his question. "Playing golf."

"With a low handicap, no doubt."

"I beg your pardon?"

He made a dismissive gesture. "Please go through everything you did when you arrived here. How did you get in?"

"The front door's never locked if someone's home."

"And it wasn't today?"

"No."

"So you came in and went straight to the drawing-room?"

"That's right."

"Did you touch anything?"

She shuddered involuntarily. "What do you think?"

"Just answer the question, Mrs. Walker."

She raised her head, meeting his eyes with an expression of dislike. "No, Chief Inspector, I did not."

"So what did you do?"

"I ran outside and called for help."

"The French windows were open?"

"Yes."

"You're quite sure about that?"

"Positive. The curtains were partly drawn; I had to push them aside to get out."

"And you called for help. You were a long way from the road; did you expect anyone to hear you?"

"I hoped Gavin might."

"Ah yes, your son. Has he still not arrived?"

She shook her head.

"Isn't that surprising when he was expected at four?"

"Not really. I didn't think he'd come; that was why I called —to check."

"What made you think that?"

"There were personal reasons," she answered coolly.

"Mrs. Walker, personal reasons have no place in a murder investigation."

"It was a family matter—nothing to do with what's happened."

"Which is also a family matter."

He saw the sudden fright in her eyes. She said tightly, "Gavin and his grandmother had a disagreement."

"What about?"

"Whether or not he should take a year off before university."

That was probably true, Webb conceded, in which case there was little to be gained by more questions. Better to ask the boy himself—when he finally showed up.

There was a tap on the door, and Sage put his head round it. "Excuse me, sir, Inspector Petrie said to tell you the gentlemen have arrived from the factory."

Ashley came swiftly to her feet. Ignoring her, Webb said, "Thank you, Sergeant. I won't be a minute."

The man withdrew. She said, "I'd like to see my husband."

"Sit down please, Mrs. Walker, I haven't finished yet. To go back, then, you called for help and Miss James heard you. Did you know she was by the pool?"

"No, but I'd heard my sister-in-law say she could use it."

He was silent for a minute, tapping his pen on the table. "Had your mother-in-law any enemies? Anyone who bore a grudge for some reason?"

"Wealthy people always have enemies. It's an occupational hazard."

"Anyone specific?"

She shrugged. "You saw the episode at the fête."

"What was behind it?"

"Dick Ridley's father was sacked from the factory for petty thieving. Three weeks later, he hanged himself."

"Had he a history of dishonesty?"

"No, but he was in a responsible position. He had to be completely trustworthy."

"And his son blames the firm for his death?"

"It would seem so."

"Very well; that will do for the moment." He stood up. "I must break the news to your husband and his brother."

"I *can* come with you?"

"On the understanding that you say nothing till I've finished."

She nodded impatiently, hurrying to the door. Webb exchanged a look of resignation with Jackson. He hadn't enjoyed the last half-hour and he wouldn't enjoy the next one. With a sigh, he followed Ashley into the hall.

CHAPTER 5

Hannah'd finished her statement, and David, en route through the hall with Ashley, had told her she could go. She was driven back to Wychwood in a police car.

Still clutching her towel, she walked up the path and let herself into the cottage. Alone for the first time since seeing the body, the memory flooded her mind with merciless clarity: the pleasant drawing-room on which violence had left its obscene stamp; the tea-trolley, its cloth spattered with blood; the crumpled, faceless horror on the rug.

She drew a deep, shuddering breath, which turned into a gasp as something soft touched her leg. But even as she recoiled, she saw that it was Arthur, come to welcome her home.

"I'll get your supper," she told him, grateful for something definite to do. She went into the kitchen, opened a tin, and divided the contents between the three bowls. She set Arthur's down in his accustomed corner and leant against the sink, fighting the sickening memories. But a moment later, ignoring the food, he again rubbed against her and, as she turned, stretched up a paw to pat her hand.

"Oh, Arthur!" Hannah said unsteadily and, bending down, she scooped him up in her arms and buried her face in his soft fur.

As the evening ground on, the machinery of a major investigation rolled smoothly into action. Renting of the church hall opposite provided them with both an Incident Room and facilities for interviews. British Telecom were already installing extra lines. House-to-house enquiries were under way, and laundries and dry-cleaners alerted for anyone handing in blood-stained clothing. Here at the house, the maid had returned from her afternoon off and been treated for hysterics; the Forensic Team had taken over from the SOCO's and the body, bagged in polythene, had been removed.

Webb straightened his aching back and watched Melanie Walker leave the dining-room.

"What did you make of that, Ken?"

"The flower bit? Didn't quite ring true, somehow."

"Read back what she said."

Jackson flicked through his pocket-book. " 'We were told at College to practise making letters.' Question: 'But why choose that word?' Answer: 'Why not? I closed my eyes and jabbed at a page of the *Telegraph,* and that's what I came up with.' Question: 'Did your father ask you about this last Saturday?' 'Yes, he was embarrassed because it had been seen from the church tower.' "

Jackson looked up. "Any more?"

"No, that'll do."

"Bit of a turn-up, the younger girl reacting like that. Not many kids faint these days."

Webb nodded absently.

"Backed up her sister on the flowers, though," Jackson added. "Couldn't budge her on that one."

"No luck with the old girl's appointment either. It's odd she never said what it was. Well"—he stretched—"that's all of them, bar the church warden and his missing nephew, and we'll catch up with them tomorrow."

According to his wife, Neville Walker had phoned at lunch-time to say he'd be away overnight; he was following up a complaint, but hadn't given details.

"Did he call back here for a suitcase?" Webb had asked. But it appeared the visit had been anticipated; Walker'd taken an overnight case with him that morning, and the phone call was merely confirmation. His wife's main concern was that he might learn the news from the papers, but Webb reassured her on that; nothing would be released till all the family'd been notified.

He thought back to his question about the "disagreement."

"Oh, at the party, yes," she'd answered absently. "The fur positively flew." Then she'd stopped, colour suffusing her face. "It wasn't *serious,* of course. Gavin's always had a temper—" And she'd broken off again, realizing, poor woman, that she was making matters worse. "O God!" she'd said, tears brimming in her eyes, "I wish my husband was here!"

But despite his sympathy, Webb wheedled out of her the facts about the cheque.

"I think Mother regretted it," she'd finished. "I'm sure that's why she asked him here today. Now, poor boy, he'll have to live with the memory of how he parted from her for the last time."

If it *was* the last time, Webb thought privately now. The boy's mother'd reacted strongly to the suggestion he might have called earlier. Had she protested too much? He moved uneasily; the memory of that interview discomfited him, forcing him to acknowledge that he'd worked off his reactions to Ashley Walker on Inspector Petrie. It was unfair and unprofessional, and an apology was called for.

He said briskly, "Right, Ken, once you've seen them off the premises, you can go. Lucky the Howard Walkers can put them up till the lab boys have finished. I want a word with Miss James before I knock off, but Harry's taken her statement, so you needn't stay. Hitch a lift back with him, and leave me the car."

Jackson made a noncommittal reply. Sometimes the Governor seemed to think him penny-wanting. This wasn't the first case Miss James had been involved with, and he'd bet it'd not be the last. And what had the old man been doing here last Saturday, if not visiting his lady friend? Still, it was no skin off his nose, and if the Guv imagined he was being discreet, Jackson hadn't the heart to disillusion him.

* * *

At their uncle's house, the Walker girls were preparing for bed. Or rather, Melanie was. Fay sat trembling, fully dressed, on the edge of her bed, and her sister threw her an impatient glance. "Come on, Fay, hurry up. I've had quite enough of today." Fay's eyes filled again. "Poor Grandma! I just can't believe it. Who could possibly do that to her?"

"What makes it worse is that I keep thinking, 'An eye for an eye—' "

"Melanie, don't!" Fay put her hands over her ears.

"Sorry, I'm as upset as you are, really."

Through the pale curtain of her hair, Fay watched her sister undress. Then, speaking quickly while her courage held, she asked the question that had been haunting her. "You don't think it was those flowers that made it happen? A kind of self-fulfilling prophecy?"

"For pity's sake, Fay! We've enough trouble without bringing in the supernatural!"

"But suppose someone saw them and got the idea? Daddy said they *were* seen, when the tower was open."

It was an uncomfortable thought, and Melanie thrust it aside. "That's ridiculous," she said stoutly. "You might just as well say someone could read about a murder in the paper, and go off and commit one."

"Some people do."

"Well, I can't be held responsible for loonies." She'd had enough grilling from the police without this, she thought resentfully, and changed the subject. "I haven't heard Gavin come in yet."

"It'll be a shock for him when he does." With a sigh, Fay at last got to her feet. "I wish Daddy was here," she said.

Hannah opened the door wearing her dressing-gown. Stepping inside, Webb took her in his arms, feeling her tremble. "Poor love," he said softly. "I'm very sorry that had to happen."

"I'll never forget it, David. Isn't that an appalling thought? It'll be part of my memory for ever."

He steered her gently into the living-room. "I don't know about you, but I could use a drink."

The low-ceilinged room, with Hannah's book face-down on a chair, looked cosy and comfortable. Webb settled into the soft cushions of the sofa, accepted the glass she offered, and patted the seat beside him. She joined him with her own drink, moving close against him.

"Can you stay? I'd rather not be alone tonight."

"Not nervous, are you?"

"Only of my thoughts."

"Sorry, love, I have to be on call, but I'll stay for a while. And Doc Pringle sent you these sleeping pills."

She shook her head. "No, thanks, I never touch them."

"This is exceptional. They'd guarantee a good night." He bent forward and put a small paper envelope on the table.

Hannah said, "Do you want me to go through it all again?"

"No, I've seen your statement. What I would be glad of are any impressions you formed about the Walkers. You did go to that coffee morning?"

"Yes, but I only saw the old lady for a moment; she looked in with a message for her grandson."

"What message was that?" Webb asked quietly.

"She invited him to tea. This afternoon!" She spun to face him. "I'd forgotten that."

"He never showed up. Or so his mother would have me believe. Was any time mentioned?"

Hannah thought back. "Mrs. Walker said she'd an appointment, but would be back by four."

So that hadn't been a fabrication. "Who else was there at the time?"

"Ashley, Pamela Tenby, and the vicar's and doctor's wives."

"Names?"

"The doctor's wife was Inez—Inez Pratt. And—Barbara Mallow."

Webb noted them down. "And they all heard the invitation?"

"I suppose so, yes."

He considered for a moment. "Was the atmosphere friendly, or did you detect undercurrents?"

"Actually I did, and Pamela Tenby told me later that Gavin had had a row with his grandmother in front of them all."

"So I heard. It would have made him a useful scapegoat, wouldn't it?"

Hannah regarded him incredulously. "You surely don't suspect those women?"

He shrugged. "Had Mrs. Tenby any other comments on the Walkers?"

"She was a bit caustic about their family tree. They go back a long way apparently and are inordinately proud of it."

"To come back to today then; you'd been at the pool about half an hour?"

"A little longer. I left home about three-fifteen."

"And you didn't hear any kind of noise till the cry for help."

"That's right. But as you know, the pool's at the back of the house and the French windows are at the side."

He nodded. "I tested it myself. You'd have been even less likely to hear a car at the front door."

"David, do you think this has anything to do with those flowers?"

"I wish I knew. It's the hell of a coincidence. I went for another look, but they'd been dug up. Walker didn't waste much time."

"But surely if they *had* any meaning, whatever it was must have already happened. He reacted when he realized they'd been planted in April. Could that be a clue?"

"There's nothing relevant on the books. I checked back, just to make sure."

"Have you spoken to the girl?"

"Yes, but she was no help. Said she chose the word at random. Strong-minded little madam—I couldn't shake her."

"And Fay?"

"Fay," Webb said slowly, "fainted dead away."

Hannah gave a murmur of distress. "So you weren't able to question her?"

"Eventually I was, but it didn't get me anywhere. And when I mentioned the flowers, she all but passed out again. She's very highly strung, isn't she?"

"She's always been quiet, but lately she *has* seemed on edge. I noticed it particularly last term."

"Exams?"

"No, they never worry her. She excels at them."

"Is she popular?"

Hannah considered. "Relatively. She has one or two close friends, but she doesn't join in much. She's not interested in sport, for example."

"I'm not surprised. She looks as though a puff of wind would blow her away."

They were silent for a while. The clock, lost in the shadows on the mantel, ticked steadily. On a comfortably sagging chair, two of the cats slept snuggled against each other. The third had jumped on Hannah's lap, and her fingers absently caressed its ears. There was a lot to be said for domestic bliss, Webb thought ironically. But he was only sampling it now because of murder most foul.

He roused himself and looked at his watch. "I must be on my way. Still, I'm booked in at the Horse and Groom from tomorrow." He smiled ruefully. "This is what I get for wishing I could spend the week in Honeyford."

"Have you any ideas at all at this stage?"

"None. Though I'll be interested to hear what the boy has to say for himself."

"It could have been a burglary that went wrong."

"So wrong nothing appears to be missing."

"You think she knew her killer?"

"There's no way of knowing. We can't even assume she admitted him—the door was on the latch. On the other hand, he might have come back with her. We need to find out where she went this afternoon and how she got home." He stood up and stretched. Hannah gently tipped the cat off her lap and rose as well. His arms went round her, and he laid his face against her hair. Too bad they couldn't just go upstairs together.

"Now, be a good girl and take those pills. You don't want to lie awake half the night." He kissed her gently. "And try not to worry," he said.

"That man," Nina Petrie said tightly, "is insufferable."

Her mother tutted sympathetically. "Drink your tea, dear, before it gets cold."

"Anyone with the most *basic* good manners would have waited till I finished the interview, but not Mr. High-and-Mighty Webb. 'I'll take over,' he says, as though I didn't know what I was doing. Quite apart from making the poor woman go through it all twice, I felt such a *fool*."

"Don't let him get your back up," her mother advised. "It's early days yet, and you want to stay in Shillingham, don't you?"

"If I could move to another office it'd help, but Lord knows when there'll be a space. I just hope I can hang on without blowing my top."

The phone rang shrilly in the corner, making both women jump.

"Whoever can it be at this hour?" Mrs. Paxton exclaimed.

Nina lifted the receiver. "Hello?"

"Inspector Petrie?"

Talk of the devil, she thought. "Yes, sir."

"Just to let you know the PM's at noon tomorrow. I've notified Constable Hobson. Normally, I'd attend myself, but in the circumstances it's more important to be at the factory when Neville Walker returns." A pause. "I presume you've attended a PM before?"

"Yes, sir."

"Very well, I'll leave it to you then. Oh, and Inspector—"

"Yes, sir?" For Pete's sake! Was that all she could say?

"About this afternoon; I shouldn't have bulldozed you aside

like that, and I apologize. It won't happen again." He paused,
but she was incapable of comment. "Good night," he said.

"Good night, sir," Nina echoed weakly.

"What is it?" Mrs. Paxton asked, as she turned from the
phone.

"He apologized. The DCI."

"Well, then," her mother said comfortably.

"It must have taken a bit of doing. Perhaps he's human after
all."

It was one o'clock when Gavin's key sounded in the door. His
parents were awaiting him in the sitting-room. Their relatives
had long since retired to the rooms allotted them, but Howard
and Ashley, in unspoken agreement, acknowledged that they
would not sleep till they'd spoken to their son. He'd been this
late before, but tonight every half-hour of his non-appearance
had increased their anxiety. Now he was here, and Howard
rose to his feet as his wife tensed, their eyes fastened on the
open doorway.

The front door closed softly; there was a quiet footfall in the
hall. Then Gavin stood there, staring at them.

"What on earth are you doing down here?" He sounded
breathless, his voice slightly off-key. "Not waiting up for me,
surely?"

"Where have you been?" Howard asked hoarsely.

"To the disco. I said at lunchtime I was going."

"You were expected at the Old Rectory for tea."

Gavin swallowed and his eyes flickered away. "Yes, well I
decided I'd had enough of that on Saturday."

"You didn't go?"

"I just said, didn't I?" He stood looking at them, palely
defiant, his hands balled into fists at his side.

"Your grandmother—" Howard began, and choked into silence.

Ashley said, "Gavin, your grandmother's dead. She was
killed this afternoon."

"Killed? You mean run over or something?"

"I mean murdered. At the Old Rectory."

He said drily, "O God." His knees buckled and he leant against the door frame. There was a brief silence, and he added, "Poor old Grandma."

"The disco was this evening," Ashley said with an effort. "Where were you this afternoon?"

"Round at Kevin's, watching a video. Then, when I decided not to go to Grandma's, I went into Shillingham, had a pizza, and met the gang at the Jolly Waggoner, and we went on from there." He frowned. "Why the third degree?"

"We've been worried out of our minds about you. You were supposed to be at the Old Rectory at four, your grandmother was murdered just about then, and there's been no sign of you since."

"You don't imagine *I'd* anything to do with it?"

"Of course *we* don't." Howard's voice shook. "But the police are bound to hear what happened on Saturday."

"And that's reason enough to suspect me? Is that what you're saying?" Gavin's voice rose. "Good grief, just because I had a slanging match with her doesn't mean I'd lay into her with a poker!"

He broke off as his mother came slowly to her feet, her eyes fixed on his face. *"How do you know that's what happened?"* she whispered.

Gavin's eyes went wildly from her to his father. Then his face crumpled, his arms went over his head, and he slid down the doorjamb to the carpet, crouching there as an onslaught of harsh sobs racked his body.

CHAPTER 6

Howard had lain awake most of the night, and he knew, from the level of her breathing, that Ashley wasn't sleeping either. Almost in equal proportions were his grief for his mother and his worry about his son, but underlying them was the old, self-castigating frustration over his relationship with his wife. It would have been of enormous comfort to them both had he been able, tonight of all nights, to hold her in his arms and make love to her; but it was over a year since that had been possible, and he knew she no longer expected it.

"Relax!" Leslie Pratt had told him. "Many men go through this at your age—it'll pass if you're patient." But he had not been patient, had demanded to see consultants, have tests, and the answers had always been the same. Nothing physically wrong—it will come right in time.

But Ashley was a passionate woman, and time might be running out. For all he knew, she had already found outlets elsewhere.

Trying not to disturb her, he turned on his side, plumping up the flattened pillow. His normal remedy for sleeplessness was to let his mind drift back over the long line of Walkers—father, grandfather, great-grandfather, stretching back in unbroken line over two hundred years. The knowledge that he was part of that line and had himself fathered a son to continue it comforted and sustained him, shrinking problems to their proper perspective.

But tonight thoughts of Gavin evoked the traumatic half-hour when he'd returned home, the tortured confession that he had indeed visited the Old Rectory and found his grandmother dead.

Howard sighed, turning over yet again. Ashley was misguided, he was sure, in her determination to keep this from the police. "He didn't touch anything—what's the point of dragging him into it?" she'd demanded heatedly.

"Since he's innocent, he's nothing to fear," Howard had reasoned.

"How can you be so naive? Once Neville's been told, it'll be national news and the police will need a suspect quickly. They already know what happened on Saturday; if we give them half a chance, they'll try to pin it on Gavin."

She'd been distraught, of course. Perhaps in the morning she'd be more reasonable, and he could advise the boy to tell the truth. Naive he might be, but he was an inveterate believer in British justice: since Gavin was innocent, the truth couldn't hurt him.

And as the remorseless wheel of his thoughts came full circle, his mother's death again overwhelmed him, and he wept silently in the dark.

The next morning, Howard and Robin left for work as usual, but the rest of the family was still at breakfast when Webb and Jackson arrived at the house.

"Dormers," as the plaque on the gate proclaimed it, was what estate agents described as "a house of character." To Webb, it looked as if it had been put together in separate portions. The walls were white, and the thatched roof swept down almost to the top of the ground-floor window ahead of them. A large dormer peered through the thatch, while to the right of the door the wall was rounded into a mock tower topped by its own conical thatch, beneath which a long, three-paned window gave onto a staircase. Beyond the curved wall, another, set-back, portion jutted out into the garden, again with a dormer window in the thatch.

"Looks like a sugar-loaf, doesn't it?" Jackson commented, as they waited to be admitted. "Wouldn't mind living here myself. Bit different from Fifteen Broadminster Road!"

Webb grinned. "You'd need a team of gardeners to keep that lot in trim." He nodded to the smooth lawn leading round the side of the house and the immaculate rockery alongside the drive.

Their inspection was interrupted as the door opened and Ashley Walker stood before them. She was wearing a coral shirt and the pale linen trousers she'd worn at the fête, as casually chic as she'd been then; but there was about her a new vulnerability, betrayed by shadows under her eyes and the almost fearful defensiveness with which she stared at them.

Webb said evenly, "Good morning, Mrs. Walker. Is your son at home?"

"Of course he is," she returned sharply. "We're still having breakfast."

"Sorry to disturb you, but we'd like a word with him."

"Very well. If you'll wait in the study, I'll send him in."

The study overlooked the sweeping back lawns. A mahogany desk stood at right-angles to the window; there were bookshelves and comfortable leather armchairs. Gavin Walker came hesitantly into the room, a youth with his father's height and his mother's good features. And also her defensiveness. Instinctively, Webb thought, He knows more than he's going to tell us. It was a gut reaction, illogical but, he felt, sound.

"I'm Detective Chief Inspector Webb and this is Sergeant Jackson," he said pleasantly. "Please sit down, Mr. Walker."

Unused to this form of address and apparently gratified by it, Gavin did so. He clasped his hands tightly together and looked up at Webb expectantly. There was silence, measured by the low ticking of the clock. Jackson flashed a quick look at the boy. This was a common ploy of the Governor's, and it invariably worked—as it did now.

Unable to bear the suspense, Gavin burst out, "Well? I thought you wanted to speak to me?"

"Oh, we do, Mr. Walker, we do. Firstly, may I offer our sympathy on your grandmother's death."

Gavin flushed and looked away. "Thank you."

"I suppose your parents broke the news when you came home?"

He nodded.

"What time was that?"

"Oh—quite late. About one, I think. I'd been to a disco."

"It must have been a considerable shock."

"Yes."

Webb hitched himself onto the desk, folding his arms and looking down at the uncomfortable boy. "Especially since you'd been expected there for tea?"

Again the flush, deeper this time, staining face and neck with hot scarlet. "I decided not to go."

Webb said mildly, "Wasn't that rather rude?"

"I didn't want another lecture," Gavin said in a low voice.

"About taking a year off?"

He nodded.

"I understand you quarrelled with her at your party?" Another nod. "I'd like to hear about it, please, in your own words."

Stumblingly, Gavin complied. His account tallied closely with Lydia's. As he finished, Webb said, his eyes on the boy's face, "It may interest you to know we found another cheque in her handbag. Made out to you, for a considerable sum."

Gavin said in a whisper, "Oh God," and his knuckles whitened on his lap.

"To come back to yesterday then. Wouldn't it have been kinder to phone and let her know you weren't going?"

Gavin spread his hands.

"As it was," Webb continued deliberately, "she left the door open for you, which would have made it easy for her killer." The boy flinched, and he went on, "You can picture her, can't you, waiting for you in the drawing-room? She'd hear a footstep in the hall, and think it was you."

"He could have got in through the windows," Gavin burst out. "It wasn't my fault!"

Webb bent forward. "How do you know they were open?"

For a moment the boy stared at him, and there was panic in his eyes. Then he said stumblingly, "My mother said so. She ran out to call for help."

"You're quite sure you weren't there yourself, Mr. Walker? You didn't decide to go and plead your case, and when she wouldn't change her mind, lose your temper? Wasn't that what happened?"

"No! I swear it wasn't! Anyway, if you found a cheque, she *had* changed her mind."

"But you didn't know that, did you? She hadn't produced it. Perhaps she made one last attempt to dissuade you, and your temper snapped."

Miserably the boy shook his head, avoiding Webb's eyes.

"I get the feeling you know more than you're telling us. It isn't wise to hold things back, you know, especially in a murder case." Silence. "Very well, we'll move on. I need to know exactly where you were yesterday afternoon and at what times."

Slowly, with a lot of prompting, they got his story. He'd been at a friend's house—"Who?" "Kevin Daniels." "Address?"—and had at that time intended to keep the appointment. But as the afternoon wore on he changed his mind, and when he left Kevin, went instead straight to Shillingham.

"By bus?" Webb interrupted again.

"No, my parents gave me a car for my birthday. I went in that."

"Where did you park?"

"On a metre in Westgate."

Damn! No checking at the multi-storey then.

"I went to a record shop and browsed for a bit. Then I had a pizza and met my friends at the Jolly Waggoner."

Times were duly noted down in Jackson's pocket-book. Gavin ended his account with his parents waiting up for him to break the news.

"And that's all you want to tell us?"

"Yes." Defiantly, he met Webb's eyes.

"Very well. Would you please ask your aunt if we could have a word?"

"You mean I can go?"

"For the moment, yes."

Lydia came quickly into the room, her lovely face gaunt. "You've managed to contact my husband?"

"Not yet, Mrs. Walker. I believe he's due back at the factory at midday."

"Yes. Yes, I just thought—"

"In the meantime, I'd be grateful for a list of the guests at the birthday party and also as many names as you can remember of people who attented the fête."

Her eyes widened. "You don't think one of our *friends* killed her?"

It was an echo of Hannah's incredulity.

"It's a process of elimination," he soothed her. Lord knew, he'd little else to go on. "By the way, where's your maid? Is she here too?"

"No, she's with her sister in Fallowfield. Poor Phyllis, she was terribly upset."

"Have you the sister's address?"

Lydia looked distraught. "I'm afraid not; we just sent her off in a taxi. I have the phone number, though, in my diary." And she hurried out of the room to fetch it.

Ten minutes later, Webb and Jackson were on their way back to Honeyford. "We'll look in at the Incident Room," Webb said, "then it'll be time to set out for the factory. I must be there when Neville Walker arrives. Except for the boy, I saw the others' initial reaction, and I intend to see his too. Then, on the way back, we'll drop in on the maid at Fallowfield."

Jackson made no comment. It would be a difficult day— interviewing people stunned by bereavement always was—but at least he was spared attending the post mortem. He was more than thankful for that.

* * *

For the second time in two days, Clive Tenby turned his bicycle into Church Lane and started to pedal up its slope, rehearsing in his mind what he would say to the Walkers. It had taken all his courage to make this second attempt; yesterday, in the first flush of his decision, he had the words pat and felt confident of a successful outcome. But halfway up the hill, a car had overtaken him and to his frustration he'd watched it turn into the Old Rectory.

He could hardly barge in if other people were there. Half relieved and half disappointed, he'd turned and cycled back down again.

So intent was he this morning on marshalling his arguments that it wasn't until he reached the gateway of the Old Rectory that he saw the police constable standing there and, on the opposite pavement, a small knot of people staring across. Frowning, he slid off his bike and approached on foot.

"Yes, sonny?"

"I've come to see Mrs. Walker"

The man eyed him with interest. "Have you now? And who would you be?"

Clive frowned, resenting the patronising attitude. "A friend of the family."

"Which particular friend?"

"Clive Tenby." His voice was sulky.

"Well, I'm sorry, Clive Tenby, but the Walkers aren't receiving visitors today."

Clive stared at him. "What do you mean? Has something happened?" He made to go in the gateway and the man moved across, blocking his way.

"Look, what is this? What are you doing here anyway?"

"I'll ask the questions, sonny. Which Mrs. Walker were you wanting to see?"

"Either of them—or both."

"What about?"

Clive said angrily, "It's private. *Why* can't I go in?"

"I think you'd better go to the church hall," the man said. While Clive watched, bewildered, the constable took out his pocket radio and a voice crackled in response.

"Stanley here, sir. Young gentleman calling on Mrs. Walker. Like me to send him over?"

The voice crackled an assent. Constable Stanley jerked his head at the building alongside the vicarage. "Over you go, sonny. Someone'll see you there."

Clive turned to look at the hall, noting for the first time an unusual number of cars parked there, including several police Pandas. He turned quickly back to Stanley.

"Has something serious happened?" God, Fay! "What *is* it? What's going on?"

The man's face softened at his obvious anxiety. "Not a relative, are you?"

Clive shook his head, even more worried.

"Well, I'm sorry, lad, I can't answer your questions. Try them over there."

Thoroughly alarmed by now, Clive swung up on his bike and cycled quickly across the road to the church hall.

Webb hadn't known what to expect of the factory. It proved to be not one building but several grouped together on the fringe of an industrial estate just outside Ashmartin. Giant letters proclaimed the name Walker & Fairfax, followed by the world-famous logo. The gate was operated by a man in a glass kiosk, who leant forward as Webb opened the car window and identified himself.

"Oh yes, sir—about poor Mrs. Dorothy. I can't believe it, sir. None of us can. You'll want reception. The white building on the far left."

Webb nodded. "Mr. Neville Walker not back yet?"

"No, sir."

"I'd be grateful if you didn't say anything till I've spoken to him."

The man nodded, relieved to be spared from breaking the

news. The bar was lifted, and Jackson drove into the yard. Several people were about, moving from one building to another or loading crates onto lorries. They had the dazed look of the man at the gate. This was very much a family business, Webb reflected, and they were all affected by the news.

Jackson drew up at the white building, and Webb got out of the car. "Keep within sight of the gate, Ken, and bring him straight in to me. I don't want anyone blurting anything out."

"What does he look like?"

Webb hesitated. "Ask the man on the gate to tip you the wink," he advised, and went up the steps into the building.

The reception hall was floored in marble. There was a fountain playing in the middle of it, and gigantic plants massed along the walls. Designed to impress wealthy visitors, no doubt. He went over to the desk. The girl there had obviously been crying. "Mrs. Walker's secretary, please." He held out his warrant card.

The girl gulped, nodded, and spoke into a telephone. Minutes later, the gates of a lift opened and a tall, slim woman came towards him. She'd have been in her forties, he reckoned, and her dark hair had threads of grey. She was dry-eyed, but from her pallor he guessed her control was precarious.

Webb introduced himself and she nodded silently. "Is there somewhere down here where we can talk? I'm waiting for Mr. Neville Walker."

"Yes, there's an empty room here." She pushed open a door and he went inside. He noted that the windows overlooked the entrance, and he could see Ken waiting by the gate.

He turned back to her. "Could I have your name, please ma'am?"

"Eunice Holt." There was no ring on her finger.

"Right, Miss Holt, I'm sorry if this is distressing for you, but I need some answers."

"I understand."

"To begin with, when did you last see Mrs. Walker?"

A spasm crossed her face, but her voice remained steady.

"Before lunch yesterday. She said she'd an afternoon appointment and wouldn't be back."

"Have you any idea what the appointment was?"

"No; I believe it was a private one."

"The note in her engagement diary said, 'B. 2:30.' Does that mean anything to you?"

"I'm afraid not."

"And her manner during the morning was the same as usual?"

The woman hesitated. "She seemed a little tense. She hasn't really been herself for a week or two."

"In what way?"

"She hasn't had her usual energy, and small problems upset her. It was as though she had something on her mind."

"But she didn't confide in you?"

"No."

"Have you been working for Mrs. Walker long?"

"Since leaving college—nearly twenty years." And at that, her voice did break. She turned it into a cough and sat calmly awaiting his next question.

"Were you aware of any hostility towards her?"

"Towards Mrs. Walker? Good gracious no. All the staff adored her."

"I believe there was some trouble recently though. A man sacked for dishonesty?"

"Oh, you mean Joe Ridley. Yes, that was unfortunate."

"Was the decision Mrs. Walker's?"

She shrugged. "It's company policy. We must be able to trust our staff implicitly."

"Did Mrs. Walker mention an incident at the fête last Saturday?"

She looked surprised. "No?"

"Ridley's son made a scene—threatened Mrs. Walker and the rest of them."

She frowned. "How very unpleasant."

Her reaction interested Webb. "Just that?"

She met his eyes, and he saw understanding come. "You think he might have followed it through? Oh no, not Dick Ridley."

A car drove past the window, and turning quickly, Webb saw Jackson hurrying after it. Neville Walker had arrived. Webb stood up. "Thank you for your help, Miss Holt. I'll contact you again if necessary, but now I must see Mr. Walker."

She bit her lip, nodded, and left the room. Minutes later, the door rocked back on its hinges and Neville Walker stood there, Jackson behind him.

"Mr. Webb? This man tells me you're the police. I don't understand."

"I'm afraid, Mr. Walker, I've some bad news for you. Concerning your mother."

"My mother?" Walker stared at him, then looked quickly to left and right as though searching for her. "Why, where is she? What's happened?"

Jackson took his elbow and led him to a chair. Automatically, Walker sat.

Webb said gently, "She's dead, Mr. Walker."

"Dead?" He repeated the word flatly. Then he said, "O God, was it her heart? I kept telling her she should ease off a bit."

"It wasn't her heart. I'm sorry to have to tell you she was killed deliberately."

Walker stared at him blankly. He moistened his lips, then he said carefully, "Are you trying to tell me she was murdered?"

Webb nodded.

"But when? How?"

"Yesterday afternoon. The weapon was almost certainly a poker."

Walker closed his eyes for a moment. Then he said tonelessly, "What happens next?"

"Your family's staying with your brother, while investigations continue. As soon as—"

The door burst open, and Howard and Robin Walker came hurrying in.

Howard went to his brother and laid a hand on his shoulder. "Nev, I'm sorry. I intended to tell you myself. I didn't know the police were here till Eunice told me."

Neville said dully, "It is true, then?"

"Yes, it's true. We'd no way of reaching you."

"I was in Stratford." He paused and added, "The Francombe business."

This was the first time Webb had seen the three brothers together, and he looked from one to another. Although they'd similar colouring, there was no outstanding resemblance. Neville, the eldest, was of the broadest build. Howard was taller and paler, though with the same light-brown hair and hazel eyes behind horn-rimmed spectacles. And Robin, the youngest, was undoubtedly the best-looking, with an underlying virility which, Webb felt sure, no woman could fail to be aware of.

He cleared his throat. "Gentlemen, I appreciate your concern, but I'm in the middle of an interview."

The two younger men hesitated, and Neville gave them a brief nod.

"Very well," Robin said, "we'll be upstairs, Nev, when you've finished."

They left the room, and there was a short pause. Walker wiped his hand across his face. "All right," he said abruptly, "let's get this over, shall we?"

"As your brother mentioned, Mr. Walker, we'd no way of reaching you. Isn't it unusual not to leave a contact number?"

Walker shrugged. "There was nothing urgent in the pipeline, and I didn't want interruptions. It was a very delicate meeting."

"Even your wife didn't know your whereabouts."

"If she'd asked, of course I'd have told her, but she doesn't usually bother if it's only one night."

"So where were you?"

"At the Hamlet Hotel in Stratford." He moved impatiently. "Look, surely all this is irrelevant now? Tell me about my mother."

"We've established that she had an appointment yesterday afternoon, but no one seems to know where. I wonder if you do?"

He shook his head. "I've no idea. Perhaps her secretary—"

"No, it wasn't a business one. Does the letter *B* mean anything to you?"

"Well, there's Barbara Mallow, the vicar's wife, but she's more my wife's friend than my mother's. I can't think—oh, wait a minute, though. Bruce Springfield. That's probably more likely."

"Who's he?"

"A neurological consultant who's an old friend of my mother's."

"Ah!"

Walker raised an eyebrow. "You think her health was troubling her?"

"Mr. Walker, I should be the one to ask that."

"Yes—yes, of course. But when you see someone every day, you don't notice gradual changes in them."

"Miss Holt said she'd been a little tense lately."

"That could be true. Well, it's easily checked. Bruce has his consulting rooms in Kimberley Road."

"Right, we'll follow that up. Had your mother any enemies, would you say?"

"Not *enemies,* that's too strong. The usual petty envies from time to time."

"How seriously did you take that incident at the fête?"

"You mean Ridley? Not seriously at all. He's aggressive when drunk, but it's all talk."

But there'd been another incident at the fête, which Webb had engineered himself. "Those flowers we looked at; do you think they could have any bearing on what's happened?"

For a moment, he thought Walker hadn't heard him. Then he said slowly, "What the devil do you mean by that?"

"Could they have triggered something off, do you suppose?"

Walker put a hand to his throat and convulsively loosened

his tie. But when he spoke, his voice was firm. "That's ridiculous. I told you, my daughter planted them; and though I grant the word she chose was unfortunate, it was nothing more than that. Anyway, they've been dug up now."

"Very well, Mr. Walker, that's all for the moment. Please accept our sincere sympathy. We'll make things as painless as we can for you all."

Walker nodded but showed no sign of moving. After an exchanged glance, it was the two policemen who rose to their feet and silently left the room.

CHAPTER 7

They stopped for lunch at the Watermill in Fallowfield, taking their beer and sandwiches out to the shade of an umbrella in the sunny garden. Sometimes, Webb reflected that his career was inextricably bound up with the county's pubs; certainly he'd patronised a wide selection of them during the course of investigations, more often than not instigated by the demands of Jackson's stomach. Left to himself, he'd have skipped lunch and pressed on with his interviews, but Ken's metabolism was in constant need of restoking and ground to a halt without regular intakes of food. He watched now while the sergeant speared a pickled onion with his fork.

"I hope you'll breathe in another direction for the rest of the day."

Jackson grinned. "Have one yourself, and you won't notice it."

"No, thanks." Webb leant back in the iron chair, gazing across the scorched lawn. It was dotted with round white tables like their own, some with umbrellas, some in the full glare of the sun. Over against the hedge, customers who'd finished eating were making the most of their lunch break by sunbathing.

High summer, he thought. The phrase was evocative of cowparsley, shoulder-high in the hedgerows, of insects droning lazily on hot, sleepy afternoons, and cottage gardens burning with the vibrant blue of delphiniums and sulphur-yellow marigolds, and out in the fields, the fragile poppy swaying among the tall grasses. He must find time to paint some poppies; he did so every year, unable to resist their glowing grace.

But before he could indulge himself, he'd a particularly brutal murder to solve. "I hope the maid's over her hysterics," he said.

She was, but her eyes were still red with weeping. "There's nothing I can tell you, sir," she said tremulously. "Mrs. Dorothy had invited Master Gavin to tea, forgetting it was my afternoon off. I offered to change it, but she wouldn't hear of it. 'I hope I can still boil a kettle!' she said. So I left the trolley ready in the drawing-room, with a cloth over it to keep things fresh."

Webb was glad she hadn't seen that cloth spattered with blood.

"Who was in for lunch, Miss Barlow?"

"There was Mrs. Neville and the two young ladies as usual, and Mrs. Dorothy'd come back because of her appointment."

"Did any of them leave the house before you did?"

"Oh yes, all of them. Miss Melanie went first; I saw her leaving with her tennis racquet. Then Miss Fay."

"Where was she going?" Webb interrupted.

"To Miss Mallow's, I think, sir. The vicar's daughter; they see a lot of each other."

"Go on."

"Then Mrs. Neville drove off to her French, and a taxi called for Mrs. Dorothy."

"What time would that have been?"

"Just after two, sir. As I was getting ready to go out myself."

So Dorothy hadn't driven to the appointment herself. Who had brought her home? Someone who unaccountably turned on her with the poker?

"She didn't mention where she was going?"

"Not in my hearing, though she did say, with that smile of hers, 'I'll be glad when this afternoon's over, Phyllis.' "

Had she been thinking of her appointment or the meeting with her grandson?

"Did you know what she meant?"

She shook her head sadly. "Is Mr. Neville back, sir?"

"Yes, we've just seen him at the factory."

"He'll be taking it bad. Devoted to his mother, he was—closer, somehow, than the other two. Poor gentleman."

There was nothing to be gained by prolonging the interview. They took their leave and returned to the Incident Room in the Honeyford church hall.

"The village is buzzing with rumours, Guv," Dawson told Webb as he flicked through the house-to-house reports. "And as you'll have seen, the press are camped at the gate. Now all the family knows, can we release the story?"

Webb nodded. "I'll give them a brief statement to go on with, and we'll have a press conference tomorrow—9 A.M. at Carrington Street. We could do with publicity now—might open up some new leads."

"There was a lad in earlier," Sergeant Dawson volunteered. "Stanley caught him trying to call on the Walkers. Demanded to know what'd happened, but we didn't enlighten him."

"Who was he?"

"Tenby. Clive Tenby."

Hannah'd mentioned the name. He'd go round to see her later. "OK, Bob. Give me his address and I'll double-check. Any of the neighbours been seen yet?"

"Yep, several that were at the party. Their statements are being typed."

"Fine." Webb glanced at the clock. Three o'clock. It was being a long day. He was hot and sticky and could do with a shower, but that would have to wait. He'd better see if he could track down the Ridley chap. No one seemed to have taken his threats seriously, but that didn't mean they'd not been seriously meant. Furthermore, according to his employers he'd not been at work yesterday.

Behind him, the Incident Room phones rang incessantly, and he barely heard them—until one call was for him.

"Would you like to take it in the other room, sir?" the switchboard girl asked. "It's free at the moment."

"Right. Who's on the line?"

"Inspector Petrie, sir."

The result of the PM, no doubt. He closed the door of the small committee room and lifted the phone.

"Webb."

"Inspector Petrie, sir, at the mortuary."

"Yes?"

"An interesting development: it seems the deceased has never borne children."

"What?"

"No question of it, according to Dr. Stapleton. She had, quote, 'a rare congenital abnormality of the uterus,' unquote."

"What about that unbroken line they're so proud of?"

"Perhaps that's why they've kept quiet about it."

"Well, it's a turn-up for the books, I'll say that. Anything else of interest?"

"Yes, she was suffering from an advanced stage of Blackett's Syndrome, whatever that is, but it didn't have a direct bearing on her death."

"OK, if you've finished there, we'd be glad of your assistance as soon as you can make it."

"I'm on my way, sir."

Webb put his head round the Incident Room door.

"What's the name of the family doctor?"

"Pratt, Guv."

"Address?"

"The Gables, Swing Gate Lane."

"And where might that be?"

"It leads down from the far side of the High Street. There's a bank on the corner."

"Has he been interviewed yet?"

He hadn't.

"Right, I'll see to it now."

Jackson was waiting in the car. He'd parked in the shade and rolled his sleeves up. He pulled them down as Webb approached, and as they set off, Webb told him about the post mortem.

"So we'll see what Dr. Pratt has to say," he finished. "There's the bank, turn down here. Now we'll have to look out for The Gables. Why don't they have numbers in the country?"

They were in luck; the doctor had just returned from his rounds, though he wasn't too pleased to see them. Probably been looking forward to a shower, poor devil, Webb thought with sympathy. Making the best of it, Pratt asked his wife to bring tea and led the way to his surgery.

Webb wasted no time. "We've just learned from the post mortem, Doctor, that Mrs. Walker never bore children."

He nodded. "I was expecting this."

"Her sons were adopted as babies?"

Dr. Pratt nodded again. Then he said slowly, "You're not going to believe this, but they've never been told."

"What?" Webb exclaimed, for the second time in half an hour.

"It's true. They don't know they're adopted. I was sworn to secrecy when I came into partnership with Dr. Sloane. Since he and old Mr. Walker died, I've been the only person who knew."

"But surely their birth certificates—"

The doctor shook his head. "The shorter form became standard when they were still children and was substituted for the originals. They never thought to question it."

There was a knock on the door, and Mrs. Pratt came in with a teatray. She was an odd-looking woman with strong, rather coarse features and she wore a tent-like dress in unbleached cotton. Webb waited until she'd gone out and the doctor had poured their tea. Then he said, "Instructions were left for them to be told after her death?"

"I imagine so."

"You never discussed it with her?"

"Good Lord, no! She was totally neurotic on the subject. Her Achilles heel, you might say."

"But *why* was it such a secret? There's nothing shameful about it."

"She thought there was. She was obsessed with the family name and the direct line going back so long, particularly since she herself was the last of the Fairfaxes. So when she discovered she couldn't have children, her world fell apart. According to Dr. Sloane, it was the only time in her life she didn't get what she wanted. Well, she offered to divorce her husband, threatened suicide, the lot. In the end, they talked her into adopting, but only Dr. Sloane and the adoption agency knew. Believe it or not, she faked all three pregnancies—padded herself, and so on. Pathetic, really."

"Incredible, I'd call it. The family's in for quite a shock. There's something else too, Doctor. Did you refer Mrs. Walker to a neurological consultant?"

The doctor folded his hands on the desk-top and looked down at them. "Forgive me, but I can't see that this concerns her death."

"Where she went on the afternoon she died is of paramount importance, Dr. Pratt."

"I see." He smiled slightly. "I'm sorry, this breaking of confidences goes against the grain. I'm glad to say I've no previous experience of murder cases. But to answer your question, yes, I referred Mrs. Walker to Mr. Bruce Springfield of Kimberley Road. I was almost sure what was wrong with her, but hoped I was mistaken. However, tests Mr. Springfield carried out over the last few weeks confirmed she was indeed suffering from Blackett's Syndrome."

The doctor paused. "Quite apart from distress on her own account, this posed a problem because it's a hereditary disease. Mr. Springfield, of course, assumed the rest of the family would be affected, but I knew differently."

"Exactly what is Blackett's Syndrome?"

"Basically, a fairly rapidly advancing paralysis which strikes in middle to old age. Unfortunately there's no known cure."

"Would her sons have known it was hereditary?"

The doctor shrugged. "When they learned what she was suffering from, they'd presumably have made enquiries. And that's one of the outstanding features of the disease."

"So," Webb said slowly, "she would either have had to let them think they were all doomed or tell them they were adopted."

"Exactly."

"Have you spoken to Mr. Springfield in the last twenty-four hours?"

"He phoned as soon as she left him."

"Did you ring back after examining her body?"

He shook his head. "I needed time to think."

"Well, that's all the medical questions for now, Doctor, but could your wife join us? I'd like to ask you both about last Saturday."

The doctor raised his eyebrows, but he went to the door and called, "Inez!"

She came, looking enquiringly from her husband to Webb.

"Would you sit down for a minute, Mrs. Pratt? I'd like you and your husband to think back to the birthday party on Saturday evening. Did anything happen which struck you as odd? Anyone behave differently from usual?"

"There was Gavin," Mrs. Pratt said. She had a deep but unexpectedly pleasant speaking voice. "He lost his temper with Dorothy, which was very embarrassing."

"Yes, I heard about that. How did the others react?"

"Much as you'd expect. Tried to pretend it hadn't happened."

"And his grandmother?"

"She excused herself and went up to her room."

"Did anyone else seem on edge? Before this happened, I mean."

"I thought Dorothy was. I asked Leslie if she was all right, but he was noncommittal, as he always is about patients."

"Anyone else?"

"Not really, except that they were trying to keep Fay away from Clive."

"Clive who?"

"Tenby. Pamela and Derek's boy. They went out together earlier in the year, then split up."

"Why was that, do you know?"

"I've no idea."

"What about you, Doctor? Were you aware of any tensions?"

"I can't say I was. My working day's spent looking for such things, but I try not to carry it into my social life."

Webb turned back to his wife. "What about the coffee morning then? I believe you went to the Old Rectory on Tuesday?"

She looked surprised. "Nothing happened there. Lydia'd invited us to meet a woman who'd come to stay in the village—a school mistress, I believe. She seemed quite pleasant."

Jackson stole a glance at the Governor, but his face was impassive.

"And everyone was quite at ease?"

"Except for lingering embarrassment about Gavin. But then Dorothy looked in and invited him to tea, so I assumed it had all blown over."

There was nothing else to be learned from the Pratts. Webb and Jackson took their leave.

Ashley answered the doorbell to find Eleanor and her son on the step, and held down a spurt of annoyance.

"I felt I had to come," Eleanor was saying. "Robin sounded so distraught on the phone. I can't tell you how sorry I am."

Where on earth could she *sleep?* Ashley wondered distractedly. Certainly not with Robin, with young people in the house.

"Come in," she said, summoning up a welcome. "It's good of you to come."

Though Eleanor must have known Dorothy disliked her, she seemed genuinely upset. Her small, cat-like face was pinched and pale, and the child beside her held tightly to her hand.

"We're just having tea. The men aren't home from work

yet." Ashley led the way to the sitting-room and through its French windows into the garden. Tea was laid on the patio under a gaily coloured umbrella. Lydia and her daughters were grouped round the table and Gavin lay reading on the grass a short distance away.

Extra cups were brought, and room made for the new arrivals. Beneath her hostess manner, Ashley wondered how long they proposed to stay. While it was a comfort at this time to have Lydia and Neville with them, Eleanor, despite the diamond on her finger, was an outsider. It was bad enough having Robin here—

She turned hastily away, lest her face betray her. Oh, *why* had she been so stupid as to get involved with Robin? Yet the answer was plain enough; her twitchy, frustrated body had been crying out for the love which Howard seemingly could not give her. Robin, an expert in such matters, had seen her need and taken steps to satisfy it. But after that one time, knowing temptation was still strong, she'd taken care not to be alone with him.

Had he told Eleanor? she wondered suddenly, and shame drenched her. As it was, she could hardly bring herself to meet his eyes; now she must also avoid Eleanor's. Then there was that policeman, she thought with increasing agitation. She'd seen his interest at the fête and felt her body respond. God, was she to be a prey to all mildly attractive men, the classic frustrated woman? It didn't bear thinking about.

"But how did it happen?" Eleanor was asking.

Lydia, glancing at her sister-in-law's flushed face, thought she understood her distress. "Ashley found her," she said, and in a lowered voice outlined what had happened. The two girls sat silently, staring down at their hands, but young Jake was listening with horrified intentness, his eyes on Lydia's face.

"Do they know who did it?" he asked in his childish voice, as Lydia came to a halt.

"Not yet, but they'll soon find him."

"But *why* was she killed?"

"Hush, darling," Eleanor murmured, but Lydia answered mechanically.

"We can't imagine. It must have been completely motiveless."

Gavin, unwillingly within earshot, pushed his book aside and lay face-down on the grass, cushioning his head in his arms. Why couldn't the little squit shut up? he thought angrily. Why did he have to keep on about it?

He'd hardly slept last night. The ghastly scene at the Old Rectory had stained his memory, and nothing he could do would banish it. Poor old Gran, to go that way. Suppose the police found out he'd been there? They had ways, hadn't they? He'd not touched anything, but his shoes might have picked up a trace of blood. It had been difficult to avoid in that first, uncomprehending horror.

And if they *did* find out, it would be all the worse because he'd lied. Mum wanted what was best for him, but Dad thought she was wrong to keep it quiet, and increasingly he did himself. O God, *please* let them find out who did it, *now,* and then he needn't be so frightened.

It was five o'clock when Webb arrived at Wychwood, and Hannah's first impression was how tired he looked. He gave her a crooked grin. "I'm taking two hours off," he said. "I'd be undyingly grateful for a shower and a meal. And if any optional extras are on offer, they too would be much appreciated!"

"Certainly, sir. In what order would you like them?"

"Shower first, meal last."

She pushed open the bathroom door. "There's a clean towel in the cupboard. Enjoy yourself."

Later, they lay side by side with linked hands listening to the early evening sounds coming through the window. Children were playing hopscotch in the lane, and a threatening yowl proclaimed that Pirate was warning off intruders.

"You want to talk about it?" Hannah asked. She was used to

CHAPTER 8

After leaving Hannah, Webb collected Jackson from the Horse and Groom, where he'd been having a meal with Bob Dawson.

"Find a telephone directory, Ken, and look up the address of the Tenbys. Husband's name's Derek, according to the guest list."

"Blackberry Lane, Guv," Jackson told him minutes later. "The landlord says it's just round the corner. House called The Thatches."

Husband and wife had been sitting on the terrace with their after-dinner coffee, while the boy desultorily hit a tennis ball against the garage.

"The police want to speak to us, Derek," Pamela Tenby announced, leading them out to the back garden. There was an undercurrent of excitement in her voice. With her nearest and dearest safely to hand, no personal disaster was foreshadowed and she could enjoy a prickle of vicarious unease.

Tenby stood up and held out his hand. "Sit down, gentlemen. Can I offer you some coffee?"

"That would be very welcome, thank you, sir."

"I might tell you there've been all sorts of wild stories flying around," his wife added. "Of course, in a village everything's magnified out of all proportion." She settled herself expectantly in her chair. "So—I presume it's the Walkers you've come about? Your men stopped Clive visiting them today. *Most* mysterious!" She smiled at Webb as though inviting him to advise her of some minor traffic offence. He had the feeling she wouldn't have been too distressed to see the Walkers taken down a peg.

Her son had moved across while his mother was speaking and propped himself against the terrace wall. He was a pleasant-looking youth, with a fresh, slightly freckled complexion. His mother's auburn hair was in his case deepened to chestnut, and his eyes, a clear hazel, met Webb's, though with a hint of defiance.

Webb spoke to him directly. "I understand you tried to visit the Old Rectory this morning?"

His mother leant forward eagerly. "What *is* it, Chief Inspector? Do put us out of our misery! Has there been a break-in or something?"

"If Clive could answer my question?"

Mrs. Tenby subsided and Clive's chin lifted slightly. "Yes, I went there."

"And refused to tell my colleagues why you'd called?"

The boy flushed. "I didn't see any reason to. It was private."

"Sonny, if the police ask you something, that's reason enough to answer."

There was a tight pause, then Clive's eyes dropped. "Sorry. It was just that the first man got my back up rather."

"PC Stanley?"

"I think that was his name."

Webb smiled slightly. "Well, in the hope that I *haven't* got your back up, will you tell me why you went there?"

Clive glanced quickly at his parents, then back to Webb. "I wanted to speak to Mrs. Walker."

"Which one?"

"Either of them." He'd said that before, Webb recalled from his statement.

"What about?" And, as the boy hesitated, he added gently, "It's important that we know, Clive."

"I can't see why, but it was about Fay. I wanted to know what they had against me."

"Why should you think they had anything against you?" He was aware that he had the parents' full attention.

"Because they suddenly stopped me seeing her and refused to say why."

"When was this?"

"At the end of the Easter term."

"Who spoke to you?"

"Her father."

"What did he say exactly?"

"Just that Fay didn't want to see me any more. I asked why she didn't tell me herself, and he said she was too upset. So I said if she was upset, perhaps she *didn't* want to break it off. We'd been out the week before, and everything was fine then." Clive frowned, remembering. "Then he said something rather odd. He said, 'You're both very young, Clive, which is why I'm making allowances.' I must have looked blank, because he added, 'I think you know what I'm talking about.'"

"And did you?"

"No! I've thought and thought, but I've still no idea what he was getting at."

Webb looked at Pamela Tenby. "Had you heard that last bit before?"

She shook her head.

"Does it suggest anything to you?"

She flushed, looking more like her son. "It sounds as though Neville thought they'd been—carrying on together."

Webb turned back to Clive. "And had you?"

His face flamed. "No, sir!" And then, "She is all right? Nothing's happened to her?"

"Nothing's happened to Fay. But if all this took place at Easter, why did you wait till now to go and speak to them?"

"Well, I was pretty peeved by their attitude. I did try to see Fay though. Several times I waited outside her school, but I always missed her. I thought she must be avoiding me, so I gave up. But when I saw her at the party, I realized I still felt the same, and she seemed glad to see me too. So I decided to tackle them and find out what was wrong." He grinned suddenly. "It sounds simple enough, but I was in a real sweat. I nearly turned back a couple of times. It was different yesterday, because I was all psyched up and—"

"*Yesterday?*"

Clive glanced at Webb in surprise. "That's right, yesterday afternoon."

"You went to the Old Rectory yesterday afternoon?"

"Well, not quite. I was half-way up the hill when a car overtook me and turned into the gateway. I didn't want to face them in front of strangers, so I came home and tried again this morning. And I still didn't make it," he added, his voice becoming indignant, "because your men wouldn't let me in."

"You say a car turned into the gate. What time was this?"

"Around four, I suppose. Perhaps a bit earlier."

Webb realized he was leaning forward, his hands gripped together, and forced himself to sit back. "What kind of car was it? A taxi?"

"No, a Peugeot 205. A red one."

"You didn't recognize it?"

Clive shook his head. "I'd never seen it before, that's why I thought they had visitors."

"Did you see who was driving?"

"No, I hadn't paid any attention till it turned in the gate." He paused, thinking back. "I'm pretty sure there was only the driver in it. But what is all this? What's so special about the car?"

Webb caught Jackson's eye, then his gaze returned to Clive. They'd arranged beforehand that Ken would keep his eyes on the parents when Webb broke the news, while he himself watched the boy.

"It's important, Clive, because at almost exactly that time yesterday, Mrs. Dorothy Walker was brutally murdered at the house."

There was a stunned silence. All three were staring at him.

Then Derek Tenby said hoarsely, "Is this some kind of joke?"

"I wish it were."

"Dorothy's been *murdered?*" his wife whispered.

"That's right."

"God, I never thought for a *moment* it was anything serious. How absolutely ghastly."

Clive's high colour had faded to pasty white. "If I hadn't seen the car, I'd have gone in," he said shakily.

His mother was trying to collect herself. "Do you know who did it?"

"No. That's why I'm so interested in that car." Webb stood up. "If any of you think of anything else, please call at the church hall." He paused, but they were still sitting in a state of shock. "We'll let ourselves out," he said.

Dick Ridley was a different case altogether. It was dusk by the time Webb and Jackson arrived at his cottage, and he stood peering out at them from the gloomy interior. He'd obviously been drinking.

"Chief Inspector Webb and Sergeant Jackson, Shillingham CID. Can we have a word?"

The man's face quivered and he made to shut the door. Jackson swiftly interposed a well-polished shoe.

"We won't keep you long," Webb said smoothly, moving forward, and the man fell back before him.

"Who is it, Dick?" someone called from the back of the house.

Webb raised his voice. "Police, ma'am. We'd be glad if you could spare a minute."

A thin young woman appeared, drying her hands on a tea-towel. "Is it about Mrs. Walker? We just heard on the news. I can't believe it; we only saw her the other day!"

Webb continued down the passage towards her, and she gestured him into the kitchen. The only light came from the grimy uncurtained window, which looked over a small, unkempt garden.

"I believe you were both at the fête on Saturday."

The woman put a hand to her mouth, staring at him with

frightened eyes. Ridley had shambled into the room after them and was propping himself against the mantel.

He said truculently, "Nothing wrong with that, is there? Open to the public."

"I also believe," Webb continued levelly, "that you were overheard to threaten the Walker family, and Mrs. Dorothy Walker in particular."

"Oh, Dick!" moaned his wife. "I *said* you should watch that tongue of yours!" She turned beseechingly to Webb. "He needn't mean nothing, sir. He was upset about his dad, and it made him talk careless. But there was no harm in it, really there wasn't."

Ignoring her, Webb addressed her husband. "I understand from your employer you weren't at work yesterday?"

He heard the woman's faint gasp, but Ridley stared at him with rheumy eyes and said nothing.

"He wasn't well," she whispered behind him. "I—kept him in bed all day."

Webb turned and looked down at her. "Mrs. Ridley, according to several statements we've taken, your husband was in the Swan public house yesterday lunchtime, and stayed until closing time."

Ridley rounded on his wife. "Stupid cow! What d'you go and say that for? Make 'em think we've something to hide!"

"Let's start again, Mr. Ridley. You don't like the Walkers, do you?"

"What if I don't? It doesn't mean I go round murdering 'em."

"You blame them for your father's death?"

The red-rimmed eyes filled. "Bloody right I do. Think they're God Almighty, the lot of 'em. All as bad as each other —the old woman, her sons and their wives. You should have seen them, strutting round that garden of theirs like ruddy peacocks! Know what they're called in the village? 'The Six Proud Walkers,' like the old song. Well, now there's only five of 'em, and that's five too many!"

"Oh, *Dick!*" said his wife despairingly.

"The pub closed at two-thirty. Where did you go then?"

"I can't remember, can I? Fair plastered I was."

"According to the barman, you were still ranting about the Walkers when he shut the door on you. Suppose you took it into your head to confront them? Complain about being thrown out of the fête?"

The man stared at him and uneasy memory stirred. Suddenly, fear spreading over his face, he started to babble. "I never laid a finger on her, sir! Never, and that's God's truth!"

"But you did go up there?"

"Never went near the place! As God's my witness!"

Webb said heavily, "We have earthly witnesses, Mr. Ridley, who saw you in the neighbourhood of Church Lane soon after three-thirty. That's the opposite direction from your home. Where were you going?"

The man shook his head. "I don't know; I can't *remember!* But I swear I could never hurt a fly! Cath'll tell you! All mouth, she calls me, but it's only *talk,* Governor, honest to God! Only talk!"

And there, for the moment, they left it.

"Nice to breathe some fresh air!" Webb commented as they came out onto the darkening High Street. "Right, Ken, we'll pop back to the hall and then we'll call it a day. And let's hope tomorrow's a better one."

The press conference was crowded, with people standing at the back. The Walkers were internationally known, and several foreign papers were represented.

"So at the moment you're treating it as a housebreaking that went wrong?" That was Bill Hardy of the *Broadshire Evening News.*

"We're keeping our options open," Webb replied. "Nothing appears to be missing, but Mrs. Walker's return might have interrupted an intruder. So that's all I can give you for the moment, gentlemen. There'll be another conference at the same time tomorrow."

As he shouldered his way out of the room, fending off further questions, the station sergeant approached him.

"Guv, there's a chap downstairs waiting to see you. A cabdriver. Says he drove the deceased home on Wednesday."

The man waiting in the interview-room turned from the window as Webb entered.

"I only heard the news this morning, mate," he began, before Webb could speak. "Telly's on the blink, so we missed it last night. Gave me an awful turn, I can tell you."

"If we could start with your name, sir?"

The man was Ernest Plover of Four Wellington Street. A doctor's receptionist had phoned, ordering a cab to collect a patient from Kimberley Road and take her to Honeyford. The call was received at five past three and he'd picked up the fare, an elderly lady, at three-ten.

"I was worried about her," he confided. "She seemed to have a lot on her mind. Found myself wondering what kind of news the doctor'd given her."

"Did you have any conversation with her?"

"No; I made one or two comments—the weather and suchlike—but she didn't seem to hear, so I shut up. I kept glancing in the mirror, but she was always staring out of the window."

"Did you drive her right up to the front door?"

"That's right, sir. She had trouble getting out of the cab, and it took her a while to work out the fare. I waited to make sure she got into the house safe, like. She snipped the latch up. I remember thinking, Good—she's expecting someone; she won't be alone for long."

"Any idea of the time you left her?"

"As luck would have it, yes—spot on three-thirty. I can be sure of that, because as I was driving out of the gate, a call came through on the radio, and the time's always given."

"You didn't see anyone else around—in the garden, perhaps, or approaching the gate?"

"Not a soul, mate."

"Well, thank you, Mr. Plover, you've tied up several loose ends for us. If you remember anything else, please get in touch again."

"So," Webb reported to Jackson over a quick cup of coffee, "we now know for certain she was alive at three-thirty and dead at five past four. At least it confirms what we've been working on."

Jackson nodded. "And as you'd expect on a Wednesday afternoon, most of the male population was at work. Except for a few unemployed and school kids, that is."

"And Dick Ridley," Webb reminded him.

"And Dick Ridley," Jackson agreed. "The cab-driver seems in the clear, since he answered his radio at three-thirty and presumably went straight to his next fare."

Webb grunted. "I'm still not happy about young Gavin; another word wouldn't do any harm. Still, before we go down, we'll drop in on the family solicitors. Parke, Ledbury & Slim— an old-established firm. They're probably not used to their clients getting the chop."

The solicitors' offices were like something out of Dickens. The overriding impression was of highly polished wood, and in the hushed atmosphere, young clerks bent studiously over their papers. The detectives were ushered into what Webb privately thought of as "the inner chamber," and the presence of Mr. Meredith Slim.

He rose to greet them, looking suitably grave. "Sit down, please, gentlemen. Can I offer you some coffee?"

"Thank you, no, sir, we've just had some."

"I need hardly tell you how distressed we all are by this terrible news. Naturally, if we can help in any way—"

"Had you seen Mrs. Walker lately, sir?"

"No, she wasn't a frequent visitor. She was content to leave everything in my hands."

"You hold her will, of course?"

Mr. Slim inclined his head.

"And any other documents for disclosure after her death?"

The man hesitated, and Webb said quietly, "I must remind you, sir, that this is a murder enquiry."

"My client lodged a letter with me some years ago, with instructions that its contents should be divulged to the assembled family immediately before the reading of the will."

"Have you any idea what it contains?"

"None whatsoever." Mr. Slim's eyes narrowed. "Have *you*, Chief Inspector?"

"Yes, sir, I believe I have." The other man would have spoken, but Webb continued. "What about the rest of the family? How well do you know them?"

"Not well. We acted for Mr. Neville Walker when he bought his present house ten years ago. And for his mother, when she sold hers on the death of her husband and went to live with him. But as a family they've never been"—he permitted himself a slight smile—"litigious."

"When do you propose to read the will?"

Mr. Slim pursed his lips. "I was wondering about that. Normally, of course, it's done after the funeral, but I suppose we don't know at this stage when that will be?"

"Not until the investigation's complete, I'm afraid."

"Quite. But I'd be lacking in my duty to postpone the will-reading indefinitely, and when Mrs. Walker left her instructions, she naturally assumed they'd be carried out immediately following her death. In the case of the letter, that might be important?" Despite himself, his voice rose interrogatively.

If the adoptions had been kept secret for forty-odd years, another week or two would make little difference, Webb thought. However, the will itself was of paramount importance, and he was anxious to know what it contained.

"I think it would be wise to go ahead as soon as possible," he said smoothly. "And in the circumstances, I'd be grateful if arrangements could be made for me to be present."

Mr. Slim looked taken aback. "Oh, but I don't know—"

"It's a legitimate request, sir, in murder investigations. Wills, as I'm sure you know, often provide motives. We might get a lead from it."

"But I can assure you there are no unusual legacies. The vast majority of Mrs. Walker's estate is tied up in the family."

"Nevertheless," Webb said implacably, and the man sighed.

"Very well, Chief Inspector, I'll speak to the family. Provided they're agreeable, I shall, of course, be happy to comply."

"Dried-up old stick," Jackson commented, when they were safely outside. "Talked like a text-book."

"He's probably affected by his surroundings," Webb said with a grin. "Right, Ken. Back to Honeyford, and we'll see what's been happening down there."

CHAPTER 9

The post fell with a plop onto the hall mat, and Hannah went to collect it: a couple of bills forwarded as requested by the post office and a garishly coloured postcard from Lanzarote. She flipped it over. Paula had written, "Weather, food, and drink perfect. Could get used to this! Hope the boys are behaving themselves, and that you're not bored out of your mind in sleepy little Honeyford."

Hannah propped the card on the hall shelf, wondering whether "sleepy little Honeyford" would ever be the same. But of course it would. Memories were phenomenally short; probably even by the time Paula returned, the worst of the horror would have receded, and its inhabitants settled back into their normal obscurity.

In the meantime, Friday was market day, and she'd decided it was time she went out. Apart from David, she'd seen no one since she was driven home in the police car, and her thoughts, continually dwelling on that afternoon, were not pleasant company.

It was a glorious morning, and as she closed the front door behind her, her spirits rose. Oswald was sitting on the gate and, refusing to jump down, hung on as she carefully opened it and slid through the gap. She set off down the lane, swinging her basket.

But as soon as she reached the High Street, Hannah realized there was no escape. The story was out now, shrieking from headlines in newsagents' racks and black-lettered on billboards, and shocked groups of women had gathered on street corners, their marketing forgotten. As she passed them, the name Walker repeatedly followed her.

Swerving away from the clutter of stalls ahead, she turned down one of the side streets and consciously slowed her pace. Here the pavements were almost deserted, and as she strolled along, exploring narrow cobbled lanes, pausing to peer in mullioned shop windows, she felt herself begin at last to relax.

This was a village of delightful backwaters and charming, unexpected corners. Rounding a bend, she came across an ancient inn, tall-chimneyed and oak-beamed, basking in the sunshine. Further along, a steep little staircase wound its way up the side of a cottage, its treads worn from centuries of use. Thankfully Hannah let the peace soak into her, strengthening her for the necessary return to the world of gossip. At the bottom of the hill, she turned and began to make her way back. The respite was over, and her postponed marketing must now be done.

At the Incident Room, Webb learned that Forensics had finished at the house, and the family was free to return. Little more had come to light. Despite the considerable amount of blood, the only trace of it outside the murder room was a faint imprint of the sole of a training shoe on the hall carpet. A cast had been made of it, and the long process of checking shoes had begun.

As Webb left the church hall with Jackson, he said suddenly, "Before we go on to Dormers, we'll have a word with the vicar. He's a family friend after all."

They walked down Church Lane to the unpretentious house immediately opposite the Old Rectory. The uniformed constable across the road straightened as he recognized them, and Webb hid a smile. Poor lad must be fed up, hanging around like that. Still, his stint was almost over.

Mrs. Mallow, small and colourless, ushered them into the vicar's study, and he rose to greet them. The Reverend George Mallow was a mild-mannered man with a permanently surprised expression—whether at the iniquities of this world or the disinclination of the next to put a stop to them, Webb couldn't decide. He had round eyes behind round spectacles, medium brown hair growing low on his forehead, and a habit, more appropriate to music-hall policemen, of rising up and down on the balls of his feet.

"Well now, gentlemen, this is a very sad business. Yes, indeed, very sad. How can I help you?"

"In your job, sir, you must keep your ear pretty close to the ground. We wondered if you knew of any vendetta against Mrs. Walker?"

"Vendetta? Oh, dear me! That does sound sinister."

"Anyone bearing grudges, ill-will, anything like that?"

"Well now, far be it from me to cast the first stone, but poor Dick Ridley does come to mind. I hear there was some trouble at the fête, though I didn't see it myself."

"We've been told about Mr. Ridley. Anyone else you can think of?"

"I don't think so. The Walkers do a lot for the parish, loaning their garden for the fête each year and making generous donations when we have need of them. Other than poor Dick, I can't think of anyone who'd wish them ill."

"You've known the family long?"

"Since they came to the Old Rectory ten years ago. Mrs. Dorothy joined them some time later."

"And they all seemed to get on well together?"

The vicar smiled. "I know what you're thinking, Inspector: most murders are domestic. Isn't that what they say? Well, I can assure you, you can discount that here. The Walkers are the closest and most affectionate family I've ever had the privilege of knowing."

"Very well, sir. Thank you for your time. We'll have a word with your wife on our way out."

"My wife?" The vicar looked alarmed.

"I believe she was at the Old Rectory on Tuesday. She may have noticed something significant to our enquiries."

"You're free to ask her, of course, but I doubt if she can help you." It was said, Webb felt, with covert satisfaction, but to his relief the vicar showed no wish to be present at his wife's interview.

Barbara Mallow received them in the living-room. It was small and neat, rather like herself, but now that he looked at her more closely, Webb realized she wasn't as colourless a personality as he'd assumed. Here, he felt, was a woman who had an existence of her own apart from that of vicar's wife. He treated her to one of his confiding smiles.

"Mrs. Mallow, your husband hasn't been able to help us much, but you ladies are much better able to gauge atmosphere. It would be a great help if you could tell us of any underlying tensions you might have noticed between the Walkers over the last few weeks."

She opened up at once, frankly and without any show of reluctance. So much for "love thy neighbour," Webb thought.

"Yes, now that you mention it, there were one or two things. No doubt you heard about the scene with Gavin last Saturday?"

"We did, yes."

"And that wasn't the only source of friction that evening. For one thing, the Tenby boy was commandeering Fay, and I could tell Neville and Lydia didn't like it. In the end, Neville asked my son to go and break it up."

"What's their objection, do you know?"

"I couldn't say. It's not as though she was too young, and Clive's a nice enough boy. In fact, having a boyfriend might give her some confidence. She's a timid little thing—spends most of her time round here with my daughter."

"Any other undercurrents?"

"Eleanor Darby," she said promptly.

Webb raised his eyebrows. "The newsreader, you mean?"

"Yes, she's engaged to Robin, and Dorothy doesn't like it. Didn't," she corrected herself after a pause.

"Let me get this straight. Eleanor Darby, the TV personality, is going to marry Robin Walker?"

"That's right. You were at the fête, weren't you? Didn't you see her?"

"I can't say I did."

"They're afraid she'll talk Robin into living in London. She's got a child too, and you know how they are about family." She paused again. "Or perhaps you don't."

"Suppose you tell me."

"Well, they're positively neurotic about it; I've always thought so. The idea of a little outsider, someone else's son, coming into the line of inheritance would really put the wind up them."

Which, Webb thought, was irony indeed, knowing what he did.

"Did they discuss this with you?"

"Not in so many words, but Lydia hinted that Dorothy was upset. They daren't say too much though, because they've been trying for years to get Robin to settle down."

"And he's resisted their efforts?"

"Up to now, yes. Between you and me, I think he's been a bit of a worry to them. Always getting his name linked with some girl or other, and nothing ever coming of it. It wasn't so bad when he was younger, but he must be nearly forty now."

"There wasn't open opposition to the marriage though? His mother didn't try to stop him, as she did with Gavin?"

"Threaten to cut him off, you mean? Oh, I shouldn't think so. That would be very Victorian, wouldn't it? And Eleanor stayed at the house and everything. I think they'd accepted it."

Webb thought for a moment. "Was Miss Darby at the coffee morning on Tuesday?" He was sure Hannah hadn't mentioned her.

"No, she only came for the weekend. She'll know about the murder by now though. Wouldn't it have been awful if she'd had to read it out? On TV, I mean. But someone else would have taken over, wouldn't they?"

She'd little else to contribute, but as Webb took his leave, he reflected he'd learnt more than he expected from his visit to the vicarage.

It was pure coincidence, in view of the foregoing, that on their arrival at Dormers it was Eleanor herself who opened the door to them. Her triangular face, with its high cheekbones and slanting eyes, was instantly recognizable, and Webb prayed that Ken wouldn't, on Millie's behalf, blurt out a request for her autograph.

"I'm afraid I'm the only one at home," she greeted them. "The others have gone for a drive, to get out of the house for a while."

"Miss Darby, isn't it?"

"Mrs., actually."

Webb remembered her son. "Of course—my apologies. Chief Inspector Webb and Sergeant Jackson. We'd be grateful for a few minutes of your time."

"Mine?" Her eyes widened. "By all means, but I can't help you. I wasn't even here."

She led the way to the sitting-room, and a boy scrambled to his feet and stood looking at them.

"My son, Jake," Eleanor said. He came forward and gravely shook hands with each of them in turn. Webb was impressed. Youngsters didn't often behave like that these days.

"Mrs. Darby, I believe you spent last weekend at the Old Rectory. We've been asking everyone if they noticed anything unusual—anything which, in the light of later events, might seem significant. I've already seen members of the family, but perhaps you, as an outsider—" He broke off, eying the diamond on her finger. "That is—"

"Oh, you're quite right, Chief Inspector," she said, "I'm certainly an outsider."

"What I meant was that somebody coming into the household might see things with fresh eyes."

Eleanor thought for a moment, and he watched her face,

DICKINSON PUBLIC LIBRARY

7688 4

framed by the sleek dark hair with its exaggerated widow's peak. Then she shook her head. "There's nothing I can think of, except the scene at the party, which everyone must have mentioned."

"No one seemed under any kind of strain?"

She gave a surprisingly harsh laugh. "Chief Inspector, *everyone* seemed under strain."

His eyes narrowed. This was something new. "How exactly?"

She glanced at the boy, curled up on the sofa reading. "Darling, this is of no interest to you. Why not take your book into the garden while I talk to these gentlemen?"

The boy obediently unfurled himself, nodded politely to the two men, and left the room without a word. If this was public school manners, Webb thought, he took back what he'd said about them.

Eleanor had begun to speak. "You asked about strain, Chief Inspector. It's hard for me to be explicit, because I'm never sure how much of the tension I sense every time I come is caused by my own presence. They resent me, you see, because I'm not a typical Walker woman."

"Is there such a thing?"

"Oh yes. The chief requirement is unswerving devotion to the family and firm. Either you work for it yourself or you support your husband, never complaining at the demands made and cheerfully entertaining boring people who might be potential customers." She paused. "At least, that's the theory. The fact is somewhat different."

"How so?"

Eleanor met his eye. "You realize, I hope, that I'm answering your questions because this is a murder enquiry and not through vindictiveness. Though when you come down to it, my only real loyalty is to my fiancé. Having made that clear, I've found they're not nearly as suave and self-assured as they seem. In fact, I'd say they were riddled with complexes, the lot of them."

Seeing his surprise, she smiled crookedly. "Lydia, for instance. Robin told me she had a nervous breakdown years ago, when her second child was born, and ever since, she's been subject to periods of intense depression. She has it pretty well under control, but every now and then you catch glimpses—and I caught one last weekend. Nothing dramatic, just a look of bone-weary sadness. It gave me quite a shock."

She was silent for some minutes, and Webb prompted gently, "You say they're *all* under strain?"

"Well, that might have been an overstatement, but I don't think all's as it should be between Howard and Ashley. Admittedly they were embarrassed by the scene with Gavin, but it goes deeper than that. They're too—careful with each other."

"And Mr. Neville?"

"According to Robin, he's had a lot of worry lately—some big customer threatening to cancel an order. Because of that, he's been sleeping badly. And as for Dorothy—well, it's hard to be objective about her. She so obviously didn't approve of me, and the rest of them took their lead from her, which I resented."

"Forgive me," Webb broke in, remembering Barbara Mallow's comment, "but will your son inherit a share of the business?"

"Good heavens, no—that was made plain from the start. Robin's made personal provision for Jake, but the firm remains sacrosanct to the Walkers."

Did she resent that? It was hard to tell. "I interrupted—I'm sorry. You were going through the family."

"Yes. Well, then there's Fay. Honestly, I think her name should be spelt with an *e.* She creeps about the place, pale and dreamy, and you hardly notice her most of the time. But on Sunday I looked up to find her staring directly at me with an expression of—" She broke off and shuddered. "I don't know how to describe it, but it was most unpleasant. Honestly, apart from Robin, Melanie seems the only one who's normal!"

And she, Webb reflected, had planted the word "murder" in

the flower-bed. It was that which first kindled his interest in the family.

"Will you be living here when you're married?"

"God forbid! It'd drive me mad. I want Robin away from here as soon as possible."

Webb looked at her curiously. The small pointed face with its winged eyebrows and sharp little chin was alight with determination. Who would win the battle over Robin, she or the family? He reckoned it was even money.

"Well, Mrs. Darby, thank you for being so frank; it's been most illuminating. Perhaps you'd tell the Neville Walkers they're free to return home; our people have finished at the house."

"What did you think of her?" Webb asked Jackson as they drove away.

"She doesn't miss much, does she? She's got them well and truly sussed out."

"It's only her opinion though, and she admits she's prejudiced. Pity we missed young Gavin. I think I'll call back later with a photo of that shoe-print. He was wearing trainers last time I saw him."

"Reckon him for the killer, Guv?"

"Could be. He certainly knows more than he's saying."

"Hannah?" Webb sat down on the bed and pulled the phone towards him.

"Hello, David. How's it going?"

"At a snail's pace. The progress, that is, not yours truly. I've been rushing round all day, and I've not finished yet. Which is why I'm phoning; sorry, but I haven't a hope of getting round this evening. I'm back at the pub for a quick snack, then I've more interviews lined up."

"Any nearer to finding the killer?"

"Not that you'd notice. We've finished at the house, and the family are moving back. How about you? Beginning to unwind a bit?"

"I'm working at it. I explored the village this morning. If all this hadn't blown up, I'd really have enjoyed pottering round."

"Ah, now that's serious; if it's interfering with your holiday, I'll step up the investigation!"

She laughed. "Good luck anyway."

If David wasn't coming, she'd wash her hair. She went into the bathroom and filled the basin, while Arthur wound himself ingratiatingly round her legs. That morning, when she'd returned from the market, she'd written a short note of condolence. Now the family was back, she'd drop it in tomorrow.

Reaching for the shampoo, Hannah reflected it was as well it hadn't been Lydia who'd found the body, or she'd surely never be able to use her drawing-room again.

For the second time that day, Webb's car turned into the drive and pulled up outside the sugar-loaf house called Dormers. The sun was just setting, and long fingers of shadow lay across the smooth lawn. This time, he was alone. He pressed his finger on the bell, thinking of the last visit and Eleanor Darby in her grey and white striped blouse. She'd seemed so calm and controlled—but was she? By now, she'd be back at the Old Rectory with the others.

Ashley opened the door, her eyes widening as she recognized him. "You again? I hear you called this afternoon."

"Is your son home, Mrs. Walker?"

She stiffened. "What do you want him for? You've already interviewed him."

"I need to see him again." He moved forward, and as she hesitated, wanting to refuse him admittance, they were for a disconcerting moment only inches apart. Then Ashley moved convulsively backwards and Webb went past her into the hall. Without speaking, she opened the study door and, as he walked inside, closed it behind him. The room was dim in the evening light, the last rays of the sun catching the corner of the desk, so that the wood glowed warm and red.

Several minutes passed. Webb walked to the window and

stood looking across the lawn to the shrubbery and low trees that lay beyond. Some starlings were refreshing themselves in a stone bird-bath, sending a spray of water over the side. In the distance was the drone of a late lawnmower.

"Chief Inspector?"

Webb turned. Howard Walker stood in the doorway, nervously fingering his tie. "I understand you wish to see my son. If you've no objection, my wife and I would like to be present."

"No objection at all, Mr. Walker," Webb said easily.

"Then if you'd come to the sitting-room—"

Ashley and Gavin were waiting for them. There was a taut, expectant air, and three pairs of eyes regarded him warily. The boy, he noted, was again wearing his trainers.

"May I see your right shoe, please?" he said, reaching in his pocket for the photograph.

"His *shoe?*" Ashley echoed, but her son was quicker. Panic flashed in his eyes, and he turned to his father, who gave him a brief nod. Balancing on one foot, Gavin took off the shoe and silently handed it over. The pattern of its sole matched the photograph exactly. Webb felt a stab of regret and impatiently shrugged it aside. Damn it all, wasn't this what he'd come for?

He looked up at the three tense faces. "You might not realize," he began conversationally, "that after finger-prints, shoe-prints are the most positive form of identification." He held out the photograph and the incriminating sole. The Walkers barely glanced at them.

"Oh God!" Gavin said under his breath.

"In view of which," Webb continued, "perhaps you'd like to alter the statement you made to me earlier?"

Ashley moved forward quickly, laying a hand on Webb's arm. "He didn't do it," she said urgently. "You must believe me—he was there, but he didn't do it." Webb ignored her, keeping his eyes on the boy.

"You mentioned receiving a car for your birthday. Was it by any chance a red Peugeot 205?"

Gavin stared back at him and slowly nodded. It fitted; it was new, so Clive Tenby wouldn't have recognized it. "Then perhaps you'll tell me the truth this time. Where were you on Wednesday afternoon?"

Howard Walker said with an effort, "I advised him not to complicate matters, Chief Inspector. It was my fault."

"No," Ashley interrupted impatiently, "it was mine. Howard wanted him to tell you. I didn't."

"Perhaps we could sit down?" Webb suggested. "It's been a long day."

"I'm sorry—of course."

The four of them seated themselves, Webb in the chair he'd sat in that afternoon, Gavin opposite him, his parents on the sofa. Jerkily the story at last came out: Gavin's arrival at the Old Rectory, finding the door on the latch, going through to the drawing-room, the unmitigated horror of the scene that met him, the blundering flight.

"I wasn't even going to tell Mum and Dad," he mumbled, "but I let it slip. And we all knew you'd heard about Saturday. To say I was there seemed like putting my head in a noose."

"What time did you arrive?"

"About ten to four—I was a bit early."

That tied in with young Tenby's statement and narrowed the margin for the time of death. What had happened in those twenty minutes between the taxi driver's departure and Gavin's arrival?

Webb got wearily to his feet. Their only concrete piece of evidence, the shoe-print, had been discounted, but he couldn't find it in his heart to regret it. "I hope you realize that between you, you've wasted a lot of police time."

Howard nodded. "I'm very sorry, Chief Inspector."

Webb looked at Gavin. "You'll be expected at the church hall first thing tomorrow to change your statement."

The boy nodded, avoiding his eyes.

"I'll see you out." Ashley preceded him out of the room. As she opened the front door she said unexpectedly, "You look tired."

"I am."

Again, briefly, she laid a hand on his arm. "Thank you," she said softly, "for not being too hard on him."

He didn't reply, but he was aware of her still standing in the open doorway as he drove down the darkening drive and turned the car towards Honeyford.

CHAPTER 10

The sun still shone as Hannah walked up to the Old Rectory, the trees made the same patterns of shade on the pavement, seemingly even the same birds twittered overhead, as when she'd come this way on Wednesday. It must seem strange to those struck down by tragedy, finding the outside world unchanged—literal proof that life goes on.

At the gateway she hesitated, looking up at the house, but there was no sign of life. She walked quickly up the drive, slid her note through the letterbox, and was turning away when the door opened and Lydia appeared, the envelope in her hand.

Hannah said, "I'm sorry. I didn't want to disturb you."

"I was on the point of phoning you. Have you time for a coffee?"

"If you're sure I'm not intruding."

Lydia stood aside, and Hannah stepped into the hall, past the table at which she'd given her statement to Sergeant Sage. Lydia said over her shoulder, "We're in the conservatory," and Hannah drew a breath of relief. She wasn't ready to face the drawing-room, purged though it must be by the attentions of the Forensic Team.

A couple were seated at the table, and the man rose as Hannah came in.

"I don't believe you've met my brother-in-law Robin. And his fiancée, Eleanor Darby. Hannah James, Fay's headmistress."

Hannah nodded and smiled. She hadn't realized Eleanor Darby was connected with the Walkers. This youngest brother was undeniably attractive, and Hannah was amused to find herself not impervious to his smile. Doubtless there'd be several broken hearts after his wedding.

She turned back to Lydia. "I'm most dreadfully sorry about what happened."

"Yes. Thank you. I don't think we quite believe it yet."

"If there's anything at all I can do—"

"Actually there is; that's why I wanted to talk to you. I'm worried about Fay; she seems to be bottling up her grief, and I don't think it's good for her."

"I hear she fainted when she heard the news?"

"Yes, but since that first evening she's refused to accept what's happened. If anyone mentions my mother-in-law, she gets up and walks out of the room."

Robin said, "Surely it's natural enough? She's hoping if she doesn't think about it, it'll go away. I feel a bit like that myself."

"Have you tried speaking to her?" Hannah asked Lydia.

"Yes, but she won't listen. She just gets that faraway look in her eyes, and I know her mind's elsewhere." She smiled slightly. "That's always been her defence against unpleasantness, even as a small child. It's most frustrating at times."

"She'll probably adjust in her own time, but if you think it will help, of course I'll speak to her."

"I would be grateful. It'd be one less thing to worry about."

Looking at her more closely, Hannah saw signs of stress in Lydia's face that she hadn't at first noticed. A death in the family was bad enough, but murder must be almost unbearable. She laid her cup and saucer down. "Is she home now?"

"Yes, up in her room, I think. It's on the right at the top of the stairs."

"I'll see what I can do, then."

The beautiful woodwork that she'd noticed before was evident on the banisters, which ended in an elaborately carved lion's head with open mouth. Hannah went up the long, shallow staircase and turned right at the top. She was about to tap on the door when the sound of singing reached her, and she paused. The song was "Golden Slumbers," and the voice so high and pure that it had an unearthly quality which sent a shiver down Hannah's spine. Dismissing such fantasies, she knocked on the door. There was no reply, and the singing continued.

Hannah knocked again, calling, "Fay?"

Still no response. She opened the door and stopped in surprise. Fay was sitting with her back to her, rocking rhythmically as she sang, her head bent over something she held in her arms. Hannah moved into the room, catching sight of a long white shawl.

"Whose baby is that?" she asked involuntarily, walking round to face the girl.

Fay looked up at her, and there was something in her glance that sent another frisson over Hannah's skin. "Mine," she said.

For a moment Hannah stared at her, then her eyes fell to the bundle in her arms and she saw with a queer jerk of the heart that it was a doll. The limpid eyes stared sightlessly; one dimpled plastic hand stretched up to the tender face again bent over it. Unaccountably, Hannah went cold.

She held her voice steady. "Aren't you rather old to play with dolls?"

Fay raised her head again, and her eyes came into focus. "Hello, Miss James," she said in her normal voice and, laying the doll on the floor, prepared to stand. Hannah forestalled her.

"No, don't get up. I'll sit on the bed if I may. Fay dear, your mother asked me to speak to you. She's worried about you." And with reason, Hannah thought privately.

"I'm all right."

"I know your grandmother's death came as a great shock, but it was to the whole family. If you share in each other's grief, it will make it easier."

Fay said with seeming inconsequence, "Do you believe in self-fulfilling prophecies, Miss James? Macbeth prophecies, they're called."

A sound at the door made them both turn, and Hannah was in time to see someone moving swiftly out of sight. She was almost sure it was Melanie. Rising, she went to the door and looked up and down the corridor, but no one was in sight. She returned to the bed and sat down again, considering Fay's question.

"I think you can be conditioned to expect things, if that's what you mean."

"Someone tells you something will happen, so you just let it?"

"Yes."

"But can it work if the person concerned doesn't know about it?"

Disturbing thoughts of black magic crossed Hannah's mind, at variance with the sun-filled room.

"I don't know, Fay. Some people believe so."

The girl shuddered. "I think I do," she said.

"Would you like to tell me why?"

"Melanie made her flowers spell 'murder,' and now Grandma's dead."

Hannah knelt quickly beside her, taking the girl's cold hands between hers as relief and compassion fought for supremacy. "Oh no, dear. I don't believe for a moment that has any connection."

Fay was hunched in her chair, her long pale hair falling forward and almost obscuring her long pale face. That something was troubling her deeply, Hannah didn't doubt. The Macbeth prophecy might be part of it, as might her grandmother's death, but there was something else as well. She said quietly, "Fay, why did Melanie plant those flowers?"

The effect of her question was startling. Fay snatched her hands away and sprang to her feet. "It was her college homework," she said, and waited tensely, fists clenched, for the next question.

Hannah said gently, "You don't have to tell me anything you

don't want to. It's just that it can help, sometimes, to talk things over."

The girl relaxed slightly. "I'm all right," she said again, but Hannah risked no more questions.

She duly reported the exchange to Lydia. "I'm afraid I wasn't much help," she apologized. And then, tentatively, "Does she often play with dolls? It seems odd in a girl her age."

Lydia flushed. "I know she's clever academically, but emotionally she's still a child. She won't let me give away any of her toys."

Hannah was turning this over in her mind as she came out of the gate, and her heart somersaulted as a figure detached itself from the shadow of the wall and moved towards her.

"I'm sorry," Melanie said contritely. "I didn't want them to know I was waiting for you. You are Fay's headmistress, aren't you?"

"One of them, yes. Hannah James."

"Would you mind telling me why you were in her room?"

"Your mother asked me to speak to her."

"Why?"

"Perhaps you should ask her yourself."

"I know she's worried about Fay, but I meant, why you?" She flushed. "Sorry, that sounded rude."

"It's a perfectly legitimate question. Presumably because Fay might feel freer talking to someone outside the family."

"And did she?"

Hannah started to move away. "You ask a lot of questions, young lady." Melanie fell into step beside her.

"Did she by any chance mention self-fulfilling prophecies?"

"I thought you heard that bit. Do you believe in them?"

"No!" The answer came too quickly.

"Specially not relating to your floral message?"

Melanie darted a glance at her. "Fay told you about it?"

"Yes, but I saw it myself. From the church tower."

"And told my father?"

"My companion did. He was intrigued." She paused. "Why did you plant it, Melanie? No"—as the girl started to speak—"don't give me that nonsense about a college exercise."

Melanie was silent, her eyes on the sunlit pavement, and Hannah added, "It was an unfortunate coincidence, to say the least."

"If I tell you, will you swear not to tell anyone?"

"It depends. Mr. Webb may need to know."

"The policeman, you mean? But it's nothing to do with Grandma! At least—" She broke off.

"So there *was* some connection?" Hannah's curiosity was roused, but they'd arrived at Wychwood. Arthur, stretched out on the sunny path, rose with his usual grace and came to greet them. Hannah said, "You'd better come in."

Minutes later, they were seated on the patio with a jug of lemonade. Hannah studied the girl's face. It was altogether stronger than Fay's, with thick straight brows and a determined mouth. Melanie came to a decision and looked up, meeting her eyes defiantly.

"Fay was pregnant and Grandma insisted on abortion. That's what I meant by murder."

Hannah stared at her, stupefied. *"Pregnant? When?"*

"In the spring. She had the op during the Easter holidays."

"But what happened? I mean, who—"

"Clive Tenby. Which is why the family warned him off."

Hannah struggled to absorb this new information. "I suppose they thought it'd be too much for her." She remembered the girl cradling her doll, and shivered. "How did she react?"

"She didn't. You know Fay. She just waited for someone else to take charge."

"I don't think Mrs. Tenby knows about it."

Melanie shrugged. "I'm not even sure Clive does. He's never given any sign of knowing."

"Who did she tell?"

"No one, I just found out. She started being sick every morning. I couldn't believe it at first—none of us could."

"You said your grandmother wanted the abortion. How did your parents feel?"

"They were stunned. And before they really knew what was happening, Grandma'd rushed it through."

"But what about Fay herself? Did she want the baby?"

Melanie considered for a moment. "I got the feeling she didn't think it would happen. The abortion, I mean. She seemed to be expecting the cavalry to gallop along at the last minute and save her."

"So she *did* want it?"

"All I know is, she cried for a week when she came home. Mummy was nearly frantic."

"And your grandmother? Did she have second thoughts?"

"Of course not. She'd saved the family name from scandal, which was all she cared about. Sometimes," Melanie ended scornfully, "you'd think she was living in the eighteenth century."

"But the abortion was for Fay's sake, not because—" Her voice trailed off at the derision in Melanie's eyes.

"Oh, that's what she *said,* but I wasn't deceived. My grandmother could be charming as long as she had her own way, but she could also be utterly ruthless."

"So neither your parents nor Fay made any protest. But I presume you did?"

"Of course I did. I made an awful fuss, but it wasn't any good. If Fay'd backed me up, we might have had a chance, but as it was, no one took any notice. They just wanted to get it over as quickly and discreetly as possible."

"Where was Fay on Wednesday?" Hannah asked suddenly, hardly believing what she was saying.

"For heaven's *sake!*" Melanie said explosively. "I thought you were on her side."

But Fay had seen the "murder" message and feared the power of Macbeth prophecies. Did she, too, believe her grandmother'd murdered her child?

Hannah shook herself. Whoever had wrought that mutilation possessed more strength than poor Fay. Unless the forcible removal of her child had pushed her beyond the brink of sanity? Manic strength could be formidable.

Melanie stood up, breaking into her gruesome thoughts, and Hannah thankfully abandoned them.

"I must be getting back. Mr. Slim's coming to read the will at twelve, and we're all supposed to be there. Thanks for the lemonade."

Hannah went through the house with her. The girl paused at the gate.

"*Will* you tell the police all this?"

"I think they should know."

Melanie gave a brief nod and set off up the lane towards home.

The stillness in the room was an additional presence, like that of the dead woman. Webb's eyes ached from concentrating on one face after another. Jackson's pen would, he knew, have recorded the poignant letter just read out. "My dearest sons," it had begun. By the end of it, they knew the term was not biologically correct.

The text was much as Webb had expected: the intention to reveal the truth, continually postponed till it became impossible to do so; an assurance of her love; and a pleading for forgiveness. However, his diligent observation, and that of Nina Petrie at the back of the room, was unrewarded. The overwhelming reaction of the entire family—and indeed of the solicitor himself—was stunned disbelief.

Mr. Slim cleared his throat, and after a quick look round the room, during which no one met his eye, he embarked on the reading of the will. As he'd told Webb, there was nothing unexpected here, which was as well, since their capacity for surprise had been exhausted. Apart from a few bequests—£15,000 for each of the grandchildren, jewellery to the wives, generous sums to the secretary and maid—the estate was divided equally between the sons. There seemed little motive for murder, and as soon as the reading was finished, Webb nodded to his colleagues and they left the house.

"So what now, Guv?" Jackson asked as they walked across the road to the hall.

"Another word with Dick Ridley. He's still about the only lead we've got."

Behind them, a car emerged from the Old Rectory and drove quickly down the hill. The solicitor, too, had made his escape. Webb wished he could hear what was being said at the house, now the family was alone.

At the Incident Room, there was a message from Hannah. "She'd like you to call as soon as possible," the telephonist told him. "She has some fresh information." More than he had, he thought gloomily. Still, it was getting on for one o'clock. Perhaps Hannah's news could be divulged over lunch.

"I'll see you back here at two," he told Jackson.

The story Hannah repeated took Webb completely by surprise. He could have sworn the Tenby boy was telling the truth when he denied having slept with Fay. On the other hand, it seemed the most obvious reason for the Walkers ending their friendship.

"I suppose it *is* true?" he asked. "You don't think Melanie made it up?"

"Why should she? Anyway, it provides a plausible explanation for the flowers."

"And a plausible motive for murder," Webb said grimly. "If, that is, the father felt sufficiently strongly about it."

"But it happened three months ago. Why would he wait so long?"

"Perhaps he'd only just found out. Clive and Fay had had no contact till the party, but they were together there; several people mentioned it. Suppose she finally told him why they'd been kept apart?"

"Would a boy of eighteen feel so strongly about an illegitimate child?"

"Who can tell? He seems a sensitive lad. And it might have been more on Fay's behalf than his own—if, for instance, he thought she'd wanted the baby."

"Discounting the moral issues, I think the grandmother had a point. Fay *isn't* mature enough to be a mother. Who knows what psychological damage it might have done?"

"Be that as it may, for a seemingly innocent old lady, Dorothy Walker roused some pretty strong feelings. Of three possible suspects—Gavin, Ridley, and Clive—two of them could hold her responsible for a death."

Hannah shivered. "I even wondered about Fay. She's been so withdrawn lately, and she was fantasizing over the doll. Also, she's superstitious about the flowers; she thinks they could have caused the murder."

"They might have given someone the idea."

"Herself?" Hannah asked fearfully.

Webb shrugged. "At this stage, we can't eliminate anyone."

"But hardly anybody saw them."

"I wouldn't say that. The church tower was crowded, remember. Any number of people could have peered down as we did."

"And thought, That's a good idea—I'll murder someone! It hardly seems feasible."

Webb pushed his chair back. "Stranger things have happened. Thanks for lunch, love, and the info. We'll have another word with the boy and see where that gets us."

But Clive Tenby wasn't at home. Webb fielded questions from his anxious mother and returned to the car. It was being a frustrating day—no discernible reaction at the will-reading and now a tantalizing snippet he was prevented from pursuing.

"We'll go back to Ridley, then, and hope *he's* available," he told Jackson.

Dick Ridley was in his grubby, overgrown little garden, dozing in a deckchair. Sleeping off a lunchtime session, Webb suspected. The garden had a depressing air. No one had troubled to water it during the heat wave, and limp leaves hung dispiritedly over scorched grass. The stench from the dustbin, with its dancing halo of flies, brought the bile to his throat.

Ridley was belligerent at being woken, but sufficiently aware of his circumstances to answer their questions with civility. Seen in broad daylight, he was younger than Webb'd thought— mid-thirties, probably, though the pouches under his eyes gave him a debauched look, and the whiteness of his skin was in stark contrast to the bright orange hair.

No, he said after a pause, he hadn't remembered any more.

"Mr. Ridley," Webb said pleasantly, "I feel I should warn you that things don't look too good. You had a grudge against the Walkers, you were heard to threaten them, and you were seen not far from their house on the afternoon of the murder."

The man stared up at him, his jaw gaping. Then, as if aware of being at a disadvantage, he manoeuvred himself to his feet. Webb waited impassively. He didn't really believe Ridley was the killer; threaten he might, but he was unlikely to have either the sureness of purpose or the cold-bloodedness to put those threats to effect.

However, Webb's tight mouth and unwavering gaze gave no hint of this opinion, and Ridley began to bluster.

"I've told you all I know, Officer. I had a kip outside the pub, then—"

"You made your way to Church Lane. You were seen, remember."

"But I could hardly stand, Governor! It would have taken me all my time to swat a fly! And I don't remember no more till I woke up on the sofa in the front room."

"What time was that?"

Ridley shrugged. "Five-thirty. Six. Not long before the wife came in from work."

"Last time we were here, you said five Walkers were still too many."

The man scuffed his feet. "Yes—well—"

"Do I take it you're still out to avenge your father?"

"I still think he was badly done by," Ridley said with miserable defiance.

"Are you proposing to do anything about it?"

After a moment, the man shook his head.

"Well, I don't want any more reports of—"

"Chief Inspector!"

They all turned as Mrs. Ridley came hurrying out of the back door. Over her shoulder, Webb caught sight of Nina Petrie.

"This young lady wants a word with you, sir."

Nina's face was white. Webb said tersely, "In the front room, Inspector," and, gesturing her ahead of him, followed her down the dark passage, his eyes half-blinded after the brightness outside.

The room smelt sour and musty. He pushed the door shut as she turned to face him.

"Well?"

"There's been another murder, sir. Robin Walker. They've just found him in the garden."

Webb swore softly. "What happened?"

"His—head was almost severed. An axe, I think."

"Very well." He felt in his pocket and handed her some keys. "Go and wait in the car while I get Sergeant Jackson."

He hurried from the room and turned towards the back door. *And then,* he thought grimly, *there were four.*

CHAPTER 11

The uniformed constable was back on gate duty when Jackson turned into the drive of the Old Rectory. Webb could see another across the lawn, presumably preserving the scene. A second murder, and only a hundred yards from the Incident Room for the first one!

"Better take a look before we go in," Webb said to Jackson. "Inspector, would you wait for us inside, please."

Nina opened her mouth to protest and closed it again. She stood for a moment on the sunlit gravel, watching the two men striding across the grass to the figure by the clump of trees. Then, with a shrug, she went into the house.

PC Hobson, older and wiser than he'd been on Wednesday, nodded at their approach. "Dr. Stapleton's not arrived yet, sir."

"All right, Constable, I'll go carefully."

"We taped the route."

Webb grunted and, keeping to the prescribed path, went into the trees, leaving Jackson with the constable. The trees were sparsely planted, slim-boled birch and ash, with some thick undergrowth between them. After a few yards they petered out, and against the high garden wall stood a wooden shed with its door open. Robin Walker was lying in front of it, and Webb's stomach gave an apprehensive heave.

Like his mother, he'd died a messy death. He was sprawled on his back, arms flung wide, one leg bent under him, with his head at a sickening angle from his body. It was all but completely severed, and the surrounding area was drenched in blood. Over to the right was a large portion of tree-trunk which had been used as a chopping block. Splinters of wood lay beside it, together with a neat pile of freshly chopped logs. The axe, seemingly carelessly tossed aside, lay in the grass, the red stains on its blade drying in the summer sunshine. The scent of warm creosote mingled with the sickly smell of blood.

"Ah, Chief Inspector," said a dry voice behind him. "Viewing the evidence, I see."

Webb turned as Dr. Stapleton came into the clearing, the police surgeon beside him.

"We must stop meeting like this," Pringle said cheerfully. "What have we this time?" He peered over Webb's shoulder at the body. "Oh dearie me. You don't need me to feel his pulse, I take it?"

Webb gave him a wry smile. Alec's macabre humour at least provided a foil to the taciturn pathologist. "As you say. Whoever attacks the Walkers makes a thorough job of it." He took out his pocket-book and did a quick sketch of the position of the body while Stapleton, taking a wide arc, moved round, examining it from all angles.

"Any immediate thoughts, Doctor?"

The pathologist frowned. "You know I don't like being rushed, Chief Inspector."

"Just something to be going on with?" Webb persisted hopefully.

The older man considered, frowning at the body. "At first glance, I'd say he was knocked to the ground before his throat was hacked."

"Which means less blood on the murderer? Just our luck." Webb turned as voices coming through the trees announced the Scenes of Crime Officers.

"OK, lads, I'll get out of your way. I'll be at the house for some time, so keep me posted."

He retraced his steps, nodded to Jackson, and strode towards the house. The little sergeant gave a quick skip to catch up with him.

"Not a pretty sight, eh, Guv?"

"You could say that, Ken, but it's the least of our worries. This second murder throws the whole thing wide open."

Bob Dawson and Nina were waiting in the hall. "The family's in the library, Guv," Dawson informed him. "All but the youngest lass and her mother."

"Where are they?"

"Upstairs. It was the kid that found him."

"What happened, do you know?"

"They heard bloodcurdling yells, rushed outside, and there she was, with the body at her feet."

Hannah's faint suspicions brushed across Webb's mind. "I'll see her first," he said. "Come with me, Inspector."

"It's the door on the right," Dawson called after them, as they started up the stairs.

There was no reply to Webb's tap, and he pushed the door open. Fay was lying face-down across the bed, threshing about and keening like an animal while her mother tried ineffectually to calm her. Motioning Nina to wait by the door, Webb went into the room, and Lydia spun round, staring up at him accusingly.

"A lot of help you've been!" she said bitterly. "How could you let this happen? First Mother, now Robin. Are you just going to stand back while we're all killed, one after another?"

Webb said quietly, "I'm very sorry, Mrs. Walker. I hear your daughter found him. What happened exactly?"

"She *found* him. With his head hanging off. How much more do you want?"

Fay's hands started tearing convulsively at her long, fair hair. To his horror, Webb saw that thick tufts of it were falling to the floor. He motioned to Nina, and she came forward, gently easing away the clawing hands and holding them, struggling, in her own.

"Have you phoned the doctor?" he asked Lydia.

"He doesn't need a *doctor!* He's *dead!*" Her voice rose hysterically.

"For your daughter." She shook her head. "Well, the police surgeon's here. He'll give her something."

He stood for a moment, helplessly looking down at the writhing girl. It was obvious there'd be no sense out of her for some time.

"Inspector Petrie will stay with you," he told them, adding to Nina, "I'll send for Sally Pierce to relieve you." Thankfully, he went out of the room, closing the door behind him.

Downstairs, he left a message for Pringle to see the girl, and sent Dawson to fetch Sally Pierce. Then, bracing himself, he went into the library, Jackson at his heels. The atmosphere was little better than in the room upstairs. Fear hung in the air. There was no question, this time, of a chance intruder, nor that their mother'd aroused specific enmity. This time, the threat was widespread and they were all in danger.

Webb's eyes went slowly round the room. It was barely two hours since he'd left it. Then, Robin Walker had been lounging at ease on the sofa, his fiancée beside him. Now, she sat there alone, her son on the arm above her, clutching her hand. She met Webb's gaze wide-eyed, betraying no expression whatever.

He cleared his throat. "I need hardly say how much we regret this second tragedy. The only consolation I can offer is that the murderer has doubled his chances of being caught."

"And when the next of us gets clobbered, they'll be three times greater?" Gavin's voice cracked, and his father flashed him a warning glance.

Ignoring him, Webb continued, "Once again, I'll need a statement from each of you. Your memories might differ slightly, and we can't afford to miss any detail. We'll use the dining-room again, and begin, please, with Mr. Neville Walker."

As they were crossing the hall, Sally Pierce arrived from the church hall.

"Relieve Inspector Petrie would you, Sally," Webb said, adding in a low voice, "Stay with the girl till she calms down; she might say something important. And ask the Inspector to start interviewing the women. She can use the drawing-room."

He opened the dining-room door and gestured Neville Walker inside. The man looked like a zombie, he thought, ten years older than the genial church warden he'd first met a week ago. In that week, he'd had a mother and a brother murdered and discovered he was adopted. Enough to age anyone.

"Please accept my sympathy, Mr. Walker," he began gently. "I know your brother's death's a terrible shock so soon after—"

"He wasn't my brother," Neville said.

Webb looked at him in surprise. Walker stared back, a blankness behind his eyes. It seemed he was still suffering from the first shock of the day; perhaps he'd not yet registered the second. Webb decided to go along with him.

"No doubt your adoption came as a shock, but after all—"

Walker's impatient head-shake halted him. "Please, Chief Inspector—no platitudes. You can have no inkling how it felt. The family simply disintegrated in front of us. I'd so much. Now, at a stroke, I have nothing. No mother, no brothers, no family."

"You have your wife and daughters," Webb pointed out. That, surely, was inarguable.

"A splinter group, a mere fragment. All this time we've been three separate units with no blood-ties, not a combined family, as we believed. Divided, we fall."

"Mr. Walker, there are hundreds upon thousands of happy adoptive families. In all but birth—"

Walker gave a harsh laugh. "Birth—exactly! Now I'll never know who my parents were. I was probably illegitimate. How are the mighty fallen!"

Deciding he'd allowed enough time for self-pity, Webb began the interview. "I'd like to hear of the events leading to your br—adopted brother's death. Perhaps you could start when Mr. Slim left you."

Walker gave his head a little shake as though to clear it. "We stayed in the library for a while, trying to come to terms with it. It was the *deception* that hurt most." He paused, and Webb waited patiently.

"Then Phyllis came to say lunch was ready, but none of us were hungry. Since the meal was cold anyway, we decided to delay it for half an hour. It wasn't put into words, but we all felt the need to be alone, to adjust to what we'd learned."

"So you split up. Where did you go?"

"Into the drawing-room. I'd avoided it since my—since Mrs. Walker was killed, but at that point I felt the need to be there."

"How long did you stay?"

Walker shrugged. "I'd no sense of time. After a while, I went out on the terrace. No one was in sight. I think most of the others had gone to their rooms."

"And then what?"

"Then I realized it was one forty-five, and went to the dining-room."

"Who was there?"

"My wife, the girls, Ashley. Soon after, Howard and Gavin came in, then Eleanor and Jake. Robin didn't appear, but we weren't too concerned." His face twisted, and he looked away, his hands rubbing hard against each other.

"When did you become concerned?" Webb asked quietly.

"When we'd almost finished, my wife asked Fay to go and look for him. We knew he wasn't in his room; Eleanor'd knocked on the door before coming down. So Fay went straight to the shed."

"Why?" Webb's voice was sharp.

"Because we thought that's where he'd be. He enjoyed chopping logs and often went down there when he'd something to work out—new designs, things like that. He said the exercise and fresh air cleared his head."

His head had been more than cleared this time, Webb thought grimly. "And then?"

"Then we heard her screaming. The rest you know."

"Who called the police?"

"Melanie ran over to the hall."

"And that was at . . . what? . . . two-fifteen?" He could
check soon enough.

"About that."

"And you'd split up when?"

"It must have been around one. That's the time we usually
have lunch."

Webb saw Howard Walker next. He and his family had come
over for the will-reading and stayed for lunch. They would not
have had rooms in which to hide away.

"Where did you go when you all separated?" Webb asked
him.

"We stayed where we were, in the library."

He was paler than ever and a small nerve was jumping in his
cheek, but he seemed less disoriented than his elder brother.
Elder *adopted*— Oh, the devil take it! Webb thought impatiently. He'd continue to refer to them as brothers.

"So you last saw your brother Robin when?"

Howard's mouth twitched. "When he left the library with
the rest of them."

"You didn't know where he was going?"

"I never even thought about it. I was too shattered by what
I'd just learnt to care where anybody went. I imagine we all felt
the same." His eyes held Webb's. "Chief Inspector, may I ask
you something? Do you think this maniac has a plan of cam-
paign or just seizes his chances as he finds them? In other
words, did he kill Mother and Robin because he happened to
come across them, or was he looking for them specifically?"

Webb rubbed his hand across his eyes. "If we knew that, Mr.
Walker, we'd have a pretty good idea who the murderer is."

Howard sighed. "Yes, I see."

"How many of you went to the scene when Fay started
screaming?"

"We all did, but Neville and I were in front, and thank God,
the women didn't see anything. We tried to make them go
back, but Lydia wouldn't budge without Fay, so Neville half-

carried, half-dragged her across. She was completely rigid and still screaming in that shrill, inhuman way." He shuddered and wiped his hand over his face.

"And what did you do?"

"Well, I—made sure Robin was dead." He gave a laugh that was more like a croak. "That sounds absurd, but you see I couldn't believe it. Only an hour before, we'd been—" He stopped, drew a deep breath. "Well, obviously there was nothing we could do for him. Gavin, poor lad, had started retching, so I took his arm and we followed the others back to the house. I asked Melanie to go for the police, but apart from that, none of us said a word. There's only so much you can take, Chief Inspector; then the defence mechanism clamps down and anaesthetises you."

And thank God for it, Webb thought. On the practical side, though, it had been a fat lot of good Hobson marking the route; it had been well and truly trampled before he got there.

"Is there any way into the garden other than by the main entrance?"

"There's a gate in the back wall."

"How close is it to the shed?"

"A hundred feet or so."

"Visible from the house?"

"No, there's a hedge in front of it, to hide the bins and compost heap."

"So the dustmen go in that way?"

Howard nodded. "Phyllis unlocks it for them on Thursdays."

"But it's kept locked the rest of the time?"

"Well, that's the theory, but the gardeners use it, and they're not as meticulous as they might be. I've heard Neville complain about finding it unlocked."

"So, providing it was unlocked, someone could have come in and made his way to the shed unobserved from the house?"

"I suppose so, yes."

"We'll check that straight away. And presumably your mother's killer could also have entered that way?"

"That's not so likely. To get to the house, he'd have had to cross the lawn in full view of Miss James by the pool."

Webb considered. "She was dozing when your wife screamed. She could have missed someone."

"But an intruder would have seen *her*. Surely he wouldn't have risked it."

There was little else of note. Webb let Howard go and despatched Jackson to arrange for the gate to be checked. If it was locked it could be discounted; if unlocked, there was an even chance the murderer'd used it to gain access. And the possibility of prints.

He sat frowning and drumming his fingers, reviewing the facts. He'd been glad enough to leave the women to Mrs. Petrie; under stress, they'd be more comfortable with her, and his summary dismissal of Nina last time was still an embarrassment. Which left only the two boys, Gavin Walker and Jake Darby.

He turned as Jackson came back into the room.

"OK, Guv, Bob's gone down to the gate. He'll report back."

Webb nodded. "Let's have a recap, Ken. At first glance, the three most likely suspects from the first murder are equally valid for this one. Clive Tenby wasn't home when we called; he could have been lurking in the shrubbery. Only question is, what would he have against Robin? Gavin, of course, was right on hand. We can't count too much on his father's assurance he was with him all the time, but again, what possible motive? Another family quarrel we've not heard of? We know Gavin has a temper."

"As for Ridley," Jackson put in, "he *seemed* to be asleep when we called, but there's no saying how long he'd been there. And he's the only one who admits to hating *all* the Walkers."

"Then we've got the family itself. According to Eleanor Darby, they're a hotbed of neuroses. Come to that, what about her? She might have found Robin'd been two-timing her, and she strikes me as a tough cookie.

"Tell you what, Ken—another errand for you: ask the Inspector to find out if anyone changed their clothes during the day. The women are more likely to have noticed, and the killer must have got *some* blood on him. And on your way back, collect young Gavin. We'll have a go at him next."

When Jackson returned with Gavin, the boy was more subdued than he'd been in the library. Had more time to think, no doubt. Perhaps he was wondering if he'd left a shoe-print *this* time.

"Tell me about your uncle," Webb began.

Gavin flashed him a quick look, then settled back in his chair, relaxing slightly. "He was a very nice guy—good fun."

"Did you get on well with him?"

"It was impossible *not* to get on with Robin."

"You didn't call him 'Uncle'?"

Gavin shook his head. "He asked us to drop it when we got to about fifteen."

Webb said casually, "I hear he was popular with the ladies." The boy was silent, and he added gently, "It's too late to be loyal, Gavin. We need to understand him, to find who was likely to kill him."

"I shouldn't think it was a jealous husband, if that's what you're getting at."

"But he'd had a lot of girlfriends, hadn't he?"

"What's wrong with that? He was a very good-looking guy."

"Anything serious before Mrs. Darby?"

"He wouldn't have confided in me."

"But you might have overheard family gossip. *Was* he involved with married women?"

Gavin flushed. "A couple, I think, a year or two back. In fact—I suppose you'll find out—he was cited in a divorce case."

Jackson made a note of the name. That opened the field a bit.

Webb came abruptly back to the present. "Where were you between one o'clock and the time you reached the dining-room?"

The boy looked startled. "You're not—" He broke off, and answered sullenly, "With my parents, in the library."

"Your mother reached the dining-room before you and your father."

"Dad felt in need of a whisky, so I went with him."

"Went where?"

"To the drawing-room, where the drinks cupboard is."

"Did you see your uncle Neville?"

Gavin shook his head. No doubt that was while Neville was pacing the terrace.

"All right, that's all for the moment. Send Jake in, will you, please."

Jake Darby looked pale and pathetically small as he hesitated in the doorway in his grey shorts and blue shirt.

"Come and sit down, Jake. How are you feeling?"

"All right, sir, thank you."

"Your mother will need all the help you can give her for the next few weeks."

The boy nodded, biting his lip.

"Were you glad she was going to marry Robin Walker?" Webb asked curiously.

The child's eyes dropped, and after a moment he shook his head.

"You didn't like him very much?"

"I don't think he liked me, sir. He only put up with me because of my mother."

"You resented him butting into your life?"

"I suppose I did, a bit."

"But he wasn't unkind to you?" Another possible motive for Eleanor.

"No, he just didn't take much notice."

"I want you to think very carefully, Jake, and tell me exactly what happened when it was decided to postpone lunch."

"Uncle Robin took Mummy's arm and they went out of the front door. I followed them. Mummy started to laugh, and Uncle Robin was furious."

"Why was she laughing? Can you remember what she said?"

"Yes. She said, 'Oh darling, you have to see the funny side, surely? All of you going on ad nauseam about your wonderful family, and all the time you weren't related at all.' "

Ye gods! "And how did your uncle take that?"

"He went bright red and dropped her arm. Then he said, 'I might have known I wouldn't get any support from you! You've never lost a chance to sneer at the family, and now when I'm more in need of comfort and understanding than I've ever been, all you can do is roar with laughter.' " The bitter words sounded oddly incongruous in the child's fluting voice.

"Then what happened?"

"Mummy put out a hand and said, 'Oh Robin, I didn't mean—' but he didn't let her finish. He shrugged her away and walked quickly round the corner to the terrace. And Mummy looked at me and said sadly, 'I shouldn't have said that, Jake. I must go and apologize. You go on up to your room. I won't be long.' So I did."

"And was she long?"

"Quite a time. I lay on my bed reading and wondering what was going to happen."

"And when she came, did she tell you she'd apologized?"

"No. When she got to the terrace, Uncle Robin was talking to Fay, so she went and walked in the rose garden for a bit. And when she went back to look for him, he'd gone. She knocked at his bedroom door, but he wasn't there either."

"How long were you alone reading?"

"I'm not sure. About fifteen minutes, I should think."

Long enough for Eleanor to have seen Robin heading for the trees and followed him.

"Thank you very much, Jake; you've been most helpful."

"Thank you, sir." The boy slipped from his chair and left the room, closing the door quietly behind him.

"And what," Webb asked Jackson, "do you make of that?"

"Question is, has Mrs. Darby also got a temper? Because if they both started shouting at each other—if, for instance, he wouldn't accept her apology—well, the axe was nice and handy, wasn't it?"

"Exactly. In each case, the murderer made use of the tools to hand, the poker and then the axe. It seems to suggest that both murders were unpremeditated, the result of sudden frenzy. And frenzy is certainly the word."

"But she couldn't have killed the old lady: she was in London that day."

Webb sighed. "Well, let's hear what she told the Inspector anyway."

CHAPTER 12

As it happened, Eleanor's statement corresponded closely with her son's. She had not, however, mentioned the scene with Robin, merely saying that he was "very upset" and wanted to be alone.

"How did she seem?" Webb asked.

"In shock. Not really accepting it."

"Think she could have done it?"

"It hadn't occurred to me, but yes, given sufficient provocation."

"Did she mention Fay talking to Robin?"

"No. I gathered that once outside the house, they went their separate ways."

"The point needs clarifying. She might just have omitted it to avoid letting on she went after Robin. On the other hand, it could be significant that Fay was with him. She might even," Webb added deliberately, "have gone with him to the shed. That could account for her hysteria."

A corner of Nina's mouth lifted. "You seem convinced, sir, that the female is deadlier than the male."

"Not convinced, Inspector, just keeping my options open."

"For what it's worth, if Fay *had* had a hand in it, she wouldn't have been as calm as she apparently was over lunch. Look how she reacted when she found him."

"Unless it was all one big act?" But after a moment he shook his head. "No, I'm as convinced as I can be that her condition was genuine. So—anything of interest in the other statements?"

"Not really. Mrs. Ashley Walker says she was with her husband and son in the library till she went in to lunch." Nina paused. "Actually, she seemed more upset than Mrs. Darby."

"Interesting," said Webb inscrutably, and Jackson flashed him a glance, remembering the interview after the first murder. He bet the Inspector remembered it too.

"And the others?" Webb prompted.

"Melanie was shocked and frightened, but she'd nothing fresh to offer. She was also upset about her sister, wishing she'd gone to look for Robin herself, as her father'd suggested."

"Why didn't she?"

"She'd not finished eating, so her mother sent Fay."

"Where was Melanie during the half-hour before lunch?"

"In her room. She felt there was nothing she could do, so decided to get on with some work."

"It's the very devil that they all separated. The only corroborating evidence is the Howard Walkers', and whether we can believe that is anybody's guess. Have you seen Fay's mother yet?"

Nina nodded. "She came downstairs a few minutes ago. Fay's been given an injection and is asleep. When they all left the library, she went to the kitchen to ask the maid to postpone lunch. She stayed for a minute or two, because Phyllis had something to tell her. I'll come to that in a minute. Then she, too, went to her room. She admitted being shaken by the adoption bombshell, but mainly because her husband was so upset."

"Um." Webb pursed his lips. "And I gather you've also seen the maid?"

"Yes; she was in an awful state, poor woman. She's been with the family for years, and it's coming apart before her eyes. As far as today's concerned, she was in the kitchen during the crucial time, but she'd made an interesting discovery.

"Apparently when 'Mrs. Neville,' as she calls her, went shopping on Wednesday morning, Phyllis asked her to buy a packet of bin-liners. She duly did so, and Phyllis put the unopened packet in the sink-cupboard, ready for the bin collection the next day. But of course, by the next day they'd all moved out of the house and she herself was at her sister's. However, when she went to the cupboard this morning, she noticed that the packet had been ripped open, and one of the bags was missing."

Webb gave a low whistle. "And presumably, in the normal course of events, there was no call for anyone to take one?"

"No, she was definite on that."

"Who knew where they were kept?"

"Lydia, certainly, because she saw to the bins when Phyllis was on holiday. But I suppose anyone in the family might know."

Jackson said, "We keep them in the sink-cupboard at home, Guv. It's a pretty obvious place to look."

"What kind of bin is it? A pedal one?"

"No, I asked her that; it's a swing-top, so it's quite large. And they've been getting extra-strong bags, since one of the cheaper ones split."

"So you could get quite a lot of stuff inside one. A shirt and trousers or a dress, for instance?"

"Easily," Nina confirmed. She hesitated, then said tentatively, "You're thinking the murderer might have stripped at the scene to avoid leaving tracks? But he could only do that if he'd something else to change into."

"Or 'she,' " Webb reminded her. "But well done, Inspector; you've a point there. He'd hardly have come prepared if it was unpremeditated—and I still think it was, or he'd have brought his own weapon. So the next question is, has anyone missed any of their clothes? Though if he'd any sense, Chummie'd have taken something from the back of a cupboard, which the owner wouldn't miss for a while."

"He might, of course, have changed into something else of his own."

"That fact hadn't escaped me," Webb said drily. "But since no one apparently did a quick change today, it seems we're still looking for an outsider. Both murders were messy, and the killer couldn't have avoided at least a splash of blood on his clothes. Added to which, the back gate *was* unlocked. It's covered with smudged prints, Bob says, which'll probably involve dabbing a bevy of gardeners and dustmen for elimination." He sighed and pushed back his chair.

"Have another word with Mrs. Darby, will you, Inspector, and check if Fay *was* talking to Robin. It'll be some time before we can ask the girl herself. In the meantime, I want a look at his room. Let's find someone to take us up."

Lydia, pale but more composed now, led Webb and Jackson up the two flights of stairs to her brother-in-law's flat. There was a large, light living-room, with an easel by the window, which Webb had to restrain himself from going immediately to inspect. In an alcove behind a curtain was a small kitchen, and bedroom and bathroom led off the landing. Much the accommodation he had himself, Webb reflected, but decidedly more plush. The chairs in the living-room were of soft hide in a deep honey colour, and there were Chinese rugs on the floor. He glanced at the walnut desk against one wall.

"No doubt that's locked, and we'll need to open it. Do you know where the key is?"

"On Robin's keyring, I should think. He always had it on him."

"Then it'll be on its way to the lab. Well, we'll try not to cause too much damage."

She gave a little shrug and turned to go downstairs. Then she hesitated, flushing slightly. "I shouldn't have spoken as I did earlier, Chief Inspector. I'm sorry."

"That's all right, Mrs. Walker. You were under considerable strain."

She nodded and went back downstairs, leaving the two men to look about them.

"The desk's the obvious starting place," Webb observed. "Like to do your Raffles trick, Ken?"

As Jackson got down on his knees, fumbling in his wallet for his credit card, Webb walked over to the easel by the window.

He found himself looking at an exquisite pastoral design in soft colours, surrounded by the distinctive gold and silver scrolling which would identify it worldwide as Broadshire Porcelain. The minute detail of petals, delicate stems, and hovering butterflies had been executed by a master, and Webb felt a rare shaft of envy. To be able to paint like that! He hoped it was sufficiently advanced to go into production, even though its designer hadn't lived to complete it.

A click behind him came simultaneously with Jackson's grunt of satisfaction, and Webb returned to the desk. The three drawers were individually locked, and Jackson turned his attention to them while Webb inspected the papers in the pigeonholes. Bank statements, insurance certificates, lists of investments, would all need to be gone through, but yielded nothing of immediate interest. Then Jackson, tugging open the bottom drawer, gave an excited exclamation.

"Look what we've got here, Guv! These look more promising!" And he put into Webb's outstretched hand some half-dozen exercise books with decorated plastic covers.

Webb opened the top one and drew in his breath. Then, as Jackson waited impatiently, he rapidly flicked through another, a grin spreading over his face.

"Well, well, well! Been saying your prayers lately, Ken? Because here's the answer to them! Nothing more nor less than a detailed account of Robin Walker's love life! Complete and, as they say, unexpurgated, as far as I can see. It'll make fascinating reading."

"Any names, Guv?" Jackson asked eagerly.

"Only initials, unfortunately. An irritating precaution, in view of the frankness of the rest of it." He gave a low whistle, his eyes racing down the pages. "If we were only looking for *his* murderer, we'd have a list of suspects as long as your arm; but I can't see how they'd tie in with his mother's death."

"Perhaps they're two separate crimes with two separate motives."

"And two separate murderers? Perish the thought!" He extracted the book from the bottom of the pile. "The first entry's dated May '78. Listen to this, Ken: 'I've decided it would be amusing to keep a record of my liaisons. It'll provide hours of happy nostalgia in my old age, quite apart from the pleasure I'll get from writing it! I can be completely frank, since no one else will ever see it, and I'll leave instructions in my will for it to be burned unread. On a more serious note, it might even be therapeutic where TG's concerned. If I can write uninhibitedly about her, perhaps the pain will go and the nightmares end. There's no doubt she's the deepest, darkest secret of my soul, and if it's to be damned, it will be because of her.' "

"Bloody hell!" said Jackson.

"What the devil does he mean, Ken? It almost sounds as if he's committed murder himself."

"When's the last entry?"

Webb flicked through the top book. "March—four months ago. 'TG again. God, this can't be happening! What should I *do?*' Then a day or two later: 'Have decided the only thing is to marry E. That should put an end to it.' " Webb looked up. "E presumably being Eleanor. I'm sure she'd be chuffed to read that."

"But who's TG, Guv?"

"Whoever she is, she's certainly long-term. He mentioned her both in the first entry, in '78, and the last, ten years later. And if she was still around in March, at least he can't have murdered her. So why does she give him nightmares?" Reluctantly Webb put the book down. "These will have to be gone through carefully, but in the meantime we can ask if the initials ring a bell. Anything else?"

"Some piles of envelopes tied together. Love letters, probably."

"Fine—we'll take them too."

"Tell you what," Jackson said suddenly, "what's the betting TG was involved in that divorce young Jake mentioned? He *ought* to feel guilty, breaking up her marriage and then dropping her. We don't know when the case was, but if she's stuck around all this time, she must still be carrying a torch for him. And marrying Mrs. Darby *would* be a way of getting rid of her."

"Rather a drastic way," Webb observed, "unless he was already thinking of it." He glanced about him. "While we're here, we'll have a quick look round, but time's getting on. We'll leave a thorough examination to the SOCO's."

The flat held no more interesting secrets. It did, however, reveal its owner as a man of taste. Webb would have liked to spend longer studying the modern paintings on the walls, the display cabinet full of the Broadshire Porcelain the dead man had designed, the interesting and well-handled books on the shelves. A life brimful of interest, only to end abruptly with the swing of an axe.

Nina was in the hall as they came downstairs. She confirmed that Eleanor had indeed seen Fay with Robin on the terrace, but did not know how long they were together. And Fay was still in her drugged sleep.

Webb looked at his watch. "It's six o'clock. I'm going over to the hall to read through these notebooks. I'd be grateful, Inspector, if you'd hang on here till Fay comes round, then play it by ear. In the meantime, you could start asking everyone if the initials TG mean anything to them.

"Ken, since no doubt you're hungry, I suggest you have an early supper and collect me at the Incident Room about seven-thirty. Then we'll go and tackle Clive Tenby about Fay's abortion. Not to mention asking where he was this afternoon."

Harry Sage was coming down the path from the church hall as Webb turned in the gate.

"Dick Ridley's in the clear, Guv, at least where the old girl's concerned. We'd a couple of blokes in earlier who picked him up at the bottom of Church Lane soon after three-thirty on Wednesday. They're sure of the time because they're shopkeepers and had been paying their takings into the bank. They just caught it before it closed, and the clerk followed them to the door and locked it behind them. They found Ridley draped over a wall, out for the count, and took him home."

"Why the hell didn't they say so before?" Webb asked irritably.

"Didn't realize he was a suspect. They let themselves in with his key and laid him out on the sofa in the front room. Then they removed his shoes and let themselves out again. That's what I call friendship!"

And at three-thirty, the cab-driver had delivered Mrs. Walker to her front door. Exit number-one suspect, not that Webb had ever really fancied him in the rôle.

"OK, Harry, thanks."

Webb went into the hall and put his head round the door of the Incident Room. "I'm going to the back room to do some reading. A cup of tea wouldn't go amiss."

In the room where, in more normal times, the vicar discussed wedding arrangements with engaged couples, Webb laid the notebooks out on the table. There were six in all—not bad, he reflected, for ten years' shenanigans. He selected the most recent, which dated from the spring of the previous year and, as he read, noted the various initials on a pad beside him. His tea was brought and left forgotten as he turned the pages.

It was indeed the journal of a Don Juan, but though Webb admired the writer's prowess, his main concern was to establish clues as to the various women who fell so easily under Robin's spell. Any of their partners could have been goaded to murder.

One point was apparent from the first: apart from the enduring TG, all the other initials were single ones. There was a B, an S, and a single T. Was the G added to distinguish the two? But TG far predated her rival. When he came upon an A, recorded just before Christmas, he added her to the list without any sense of significance. But as he went on, suspicion grew, and he leafed back and read it again more carefully.

"Think I might be in with a chance with A. She's very

jumpy at the moment, and when on the offchance I treated her to one of my looks, she went gratifyingly red. Fingers crossed!"

And again, some days later: "A's definitely ripe for the plucking. Can't think how this has happened, but who am I to question it? Feel a bit of a heel regarding H, but if she's that way inclined, we might as well keep it in the family."

In the family! There was the proof. Ashley Walker—and Howard! In his head, Nina's voice repeated, "She seemed more upset than Mrs. Darby."

Then came the triumphant entry "Landed A last night. An all-time high. Tears of remorse afterwards, but only to be expected. Gather she and H haven't been getting it right lately and she's a lady who needs her oats. Positively no complaints on either side!" Did Howard know he'd been cuckolded by his younger brother? If so, how would he have reacted?

But she would not be caught a second time. Perhaps the remorse was genuine. Robin pursued her for a while without success, then A disappeared from the page as E gained prominence.

Webb owned himself surprised. Ashley Walker had not struck him as someone who'd play around in her own backyard. But Robin hinted she was frustrated. Which, Webb thought, growing hot, could explain her scrutiny of himself at the fête.

A knock at the door was a welcome diversion. One of the typists stood there, a plate in her hand. "We've just made sandwiches, sir, and wondered if you'd like some?"

"Thanks," Webb said gratefully, "I should."

"Cheese and pickle all right?"

"Perfect. And I let my last cup of tea get cold. Any chance of another?"

"Of course, sir."

By the time Jackson called for him as arranged, Webb had finished the notebook and was staring broodily at the list of initials on his pad.

"Trouble is, Ken, our Robin got about a fair bit. He often

went abroad on business and spent a lot of time in London, which was where he met Eleanor."

"So his conquests are quite spread out?"

"Exactly, including several one-night stands. Sometimes he refers to the location, sometimes not. It'll be like a needle in a haystack tracking down this lot."

Except, he conceded silently, for Ashley and Howard Walker. He'd not yet decided how to make use of that knowledge and in the meantime was keeping his own counsel.

"Are you ready to see young Tenby, then?"

Webb nodded, stretched, and got to his feet. "Let's see what he has to tell us."

They arrived at the house to find Mr. and Mrs. Tenby out and Clive entertaining friends. The sounds of the stereo greeted them as they got out of the car, and through the sitting-room window, they could see couples gyrating around.

Clive himself flung open the door, obviously expecting more of his guests. He looked taken aback to see them, but not alarmed.

"Yes, Chief Inspector?" he said warily.

"Sorry to interrupt your party, but we'd like a word with you."

"OK—come in."

The house was throbbing with the beat of the music—not quite the atmosphere in which to talk of death and abortion.

Clive said apologetically, "The dining-room should be fairly quiet," and led them to the room on the far side of the house, closing the door behind him. At least the noise was muted here. Webb cleared his throat.

"I have two pieces of news for you—if, indeed, they are news. But first, would you tell me, please, where you were around lunch-time today?"

"Oh yes, my mother said you called. We'd gone over to the Plough at Fallowfield for a pub lunch. We often do on Saturdays."

"Who's 'we'?"

"A group of friends and myself."

"What time did you leave here?"

Clive shrugged. "Around twelve-thirty."

"And you got back when?"

"Not till after four. We went for a long walk through the woods."

"You were with your friends the whole time?"

"Yes." Clive looked puzzled. "You said you had some news, Chief Inspector?"

For the second time, Webb informed him of a violent death in the Walker family. Clive stared at him in horror.

"*Robin?* I can't *believe* it! Who'd want to kill him?"

"That, my lad, is what we intend to find out."

"Well, it wasn't me!" Clive said hotly. Then, as Webb made no comment, "You said there were two things?"

"Ah yes." Webb paused, his eyes on the boy's face. "Are you aware that Fay Walker had an abortion last April?"

Clive blinked convulsively, as though he'd been physically struck. Then colour suffused his face and he said in a strangled voice, "That's a dirty lie!"

"No, it's the truth. I ask you again if you slept with her."

"And I tell you again, no! And there was no one else, if that's what you're thinking. We were going out together; don't you think I'd have known?"

His shock was obviously genuine, and Webb felt sympathy for him. "Nevertheless, we can't argue with facts." He paused. "Wasn't it about then that your friendship ended?"

"You're saying *that* was why? They thought it was mine? But of course, they would. Why didn't she *tell* them?" Then the answer seemed to come to him. "She must have been raped! Poor girl—she'd have been too ashamed to say anything."

It was possible, Webb conceded. According to Melanie, the family had no doubt the child was Clive's, but Fay had never confirmed it. If indeed she'd been raped, it would dispose of the father as a possible murder suspect.

Warming to his solution, Clive went on, "Believe me, Chief

Inspector, it must have been that. I *know* she wouldn't have gone with anyone else. She's not that kind of girl." And from his own observance of Fay, Webb was inclined to agree.

"God, what she must have gone through! Why didn't she *tell* me?"

"I can't answer that, I'm afraid. Well, we won't keep you from your friends any longer."

In silence, Clive led them to the front door. Their last sight of him was his stiff figure in the doorway being suddenly swallowed up by a wave of laughing, glass-waving party-goers.

CHAPTER 13

They sat in the car outside the Tenbys' house for several minutes, reviewing the last few hours. Webb's sense of urgency was deepening. After this second murder, there must, surely, be a collective danger for the entire family; it was inconceivable that two members of it could be singled out within the space of three days for entirely separate reasons. It was also depressingly obvious that the strong police presence had not proved a deterrent. No wonder the family was frightened and resentful.

Eventually he straightened and looked at his watch. "Well, this isn't getting us anywhere; better to come to it fresh tomorrow. It's been quite a day—press conference, will-reading, murder—and those are just the high spots.

"Once more job, though, before you knock off. Look in at the Old Rectory and check with Sally if the girl's come round and said anything. Then split the adults between you and Inspector Petrie, and see what they know about this divorce case. If by any chance TG was involved, it could be of interest. After that, all three of you are free to go home. Two of our blokes will be in the house overnight and another two in the grounds, and the same goes for Dormers. No saying who might be next on the list."

Jackson nodded. "Shall I leave you the car, Guv?"

"Yes; I've a couple of things to check, then I'll call it a day myself. Hang on—" He reached into the back of the car and retrieved a couple of the notebooks he'd not had time to look at. "Here's some bedtime reading for you."

As Jackson got out of the car, the strains of music from the party reached them again. Webb wondered if Clive had been

able to push what he'd learned to the back of his mind. Judging
by his initial response, he doubted it. He watched Jackson's
slight figure set off up the hill. Then, decision crystallizing, he
drove down to the main road and turned right in the direction
of Dormers. The Howard Walkers should be home by now.

Ashley stood at the long window on the half-landing, staring
down the driveway. She was not sure why she was there; she'd
taken some aspirin and hot milk to Howard, who'd been
stricken with a severe migraine, and on her way downstairs had
glanced out of the window, paused, and then remained there,
suddenly unwilling to continue to the ground floor. It was in
any case deserted, except for the two polite strangers who'd
settled in the study for the night.

Gavin was at a pop concert, to which he'd been looking
forward for weeks. There'd been no point in suggesting he
should cancel it; Robin wouldn't be helped by his staying miserably at home. Robin wouldn't be helped by anything, ever
again.

Her throat closed over a dry sob, remembering him as he'd
been only that afternoon, with his arm carelessly along the
back of the sofa behind Eleanor, his face mirroring the shock
they'd all felt. Remembering, too, his tenderness when they'd
made love.

Her eyes, still fixed unseeingly on the drive, flickered into
focus as a car turned in at the gate. Immediately, a figure
materialised from behind a bush and bent its head to speak to
the driver. Then it stepped back, and the car came on towards
the house. A sanctioned visitor, then. She stood unmoving as
Webb got out of the car and, drawn perhaps by the force of her
gaze, glanced up at the window in the low turret where she
stood. For a moment they stared at each other. Then he came
on towards the house and she walked down the remaining
stairs, gathering together the shreds of her self-control.

One of the policemen reached the door before her and admitted Webb. Perhaps his colleague outside had radioed news of

his arrival. After a murmured consultation, he returned to the study and closed the door.

Ashley said, "My husband's in bed and can't be disturbed. Not surprisingly, he has a bad headache."

"I'm sorry."

"For that matter, I'm in no state to be interviewed either. I thought we'd finished with all that at the Old Rectory."

"Unfortunately some more questions have come up."

She turned on her heel and led the way to the sitting-room. The evening had clouded over and it was dim in the long, low room, but she made no move to switch on the light. Nor did she invite him to sit, and they stood facing each other like boxers in a ring. Her scent hung faintly in the air, disturbingly seductive. Webb cleared his throat. "Are you aware that Robin Walker kept a diary?"

A tremor went through her, but she answered contemptuously, "And you've been smacking your lips over it, no doubt?"

"Mrs. Walker, please understand I'm only—"

"Only what?" she broke in furiously. "Doing your duty? Spare me that!"

"It happens to be true."

"Rubbish! You're enjoying seeing us get our comeuppance—isn't that how you regard it? The high and mighty Walkers brought low? How *dare* you set yourself up like a little tin god to poke into our affairs! Go away, and leave us to mourn our dead."

Webb said doggedly, "Did your husband know of your relationship with his brother?"

She stepped forward swiftly, hand raised, and he caught and held her wrist. "Because if he did," Webb continued, as she stood glaring at him, "it might constitute a motive for murder."

He felt her go limp and tightened his grip to support her. "Mrs. Walker," he said more gently, "whatever you may think, I'm not enjoying this any more than you are."

"You make it sound so sordid," she answered in a low voice. "It wasn't—and it only happened once."

"I know."

Her head reared. "God, you're insufferable! Is there anything you *don't* know? But whatever views you might have of me, I don't sleep around. That one occasion with Robin, which I've bitterly regretted, was the only time in—" She broke off. "Why am I telling you this? It's none of your damn business."

"Did your husband find out?" Webb repeated, releasing her wrist.

"No, I'm sure he didn't. I'd have known. Look, this is ludicrous. You're not casting *Howard* in the rôle of murderer?"

"Who would you suggest?"

She stared at him and gave a little shiver. "I've tried to avoid thinking it could be someone we know."

"The second murder makes it increasingly likely. Is there anyone, apart from Ridley, who feels wronged by the family?"

"Connected with the firm, you mean?"

"Quite possibly. I'm going back on Monday, to make enquiries. It could be a business rather than a personal vendetta." Though for all he knew, TG might be employed there. It would explain the long-lasting relationship.

"Are you expecting another attack?" Ashley asked fearfully.

"We're taking no chances." He hesitated, wondering how best to phrase his next question.

"I have the impression Mrs. Darby's not too popular?"

His tact was wasted. "You mean did I resent her being Robin's fiancée?"

"That's part of it, but I hear your mother-in-law didn't welcome her either."

"She was too independent for Mother's liking."

"And for yours?"

"I've nothing against her." Even in these circumstances, she was unwilling to discuss the family. And yet, standing close to her in the gathering dusk, he sensed a softening of her antagonism, perhaps a more personal awareness. Which could be dangerous.

She said quietly, "If you've finished interrogating me, shall we be civilised and have a drink?"

How to refuse without offending her? For refuse he must; every instinct demanded it. He was literally saved by the bell—the telephone, which shrilled suddenly across the room. The couple of minutes during which she spoke into it gave him time to collect himself, and as she put it down, he said smoothly, "Thank you, but I must be on my way."

"Perhaps you're right," she said.

She saw him to the door and held it open as he walked briskly to the car. Then it closed, and the light illuminating the gravel was extinguished. With a sigh he didn't entirely understand, he switched on the ignition.

Hannah said, *"Robin?* But he *can't* be! I saw him this morning!"

"Unfortunately, my love, that's no guarantee of immortality." Webb poured whisky into two glasses, diluted hers with dry ginger.

"But David, that's horrible!" She was still gazing at him in distress. "Every time I go to that house, someone is killed."

"Then please don't go again," he said grimly, handing her the glass. "Think back to the coffee morning. Or the fête, for that matter. Do you recall anyone being spoken of who had the initials TG?"

"I don't think so," Hannah said after a moment. "Why?"

"Because Robin kept a record of his amorous exploits, and those initials figured over a long period."

"And you think a jealous husband came after him? But what about his mother?"

Webb settled himself in a deep armchair and stared reflectively into his drink. "TG was something special. Not only did she outlast all the others; he referred to her as the deepest and darkest secret of his soul."

"Good Lord!"

"It's possible that, in the end, she was the cause of his death. But, as you so rightly say, what about his mother?"

Hannah said slowly, "If Eleanor Darby'd found out—"

"We wondered about that, but to be honest, I doubt if she'd have cared sufficiently. However, she and Robin did have words after the will-reading. She went after him to apologize, but he was talking to Fay, so she left it."

"And that was the last time she saw him?"

"So she says. It was Fay who found him. She knew where to look, but it seems he often went to chop wood when he'd problems to sort out."

"How's Fay now?"

"Under sedation. She was having screaming hysterics when I saw her."

Hannah said gravely, "It's enough to tip her over the edge. She's been more and more withdrawn . . . well, I told you about the doll. Heavens, was that only this morning?"

"You know her better than I do; is it conceivable she could have killed Robin herself? She was, after all, the last person seen with him."

"Would she have had the strength?"

"Manic fury? If he was taken by surprise—" He slapped the arm of his chair with frustration. "If I was at home, I'd have the easel up by now. The killer *has* to be one of a closed circle of people. What are we missing?"

"I haven't an easel, but I can supply pen and paper, if that's any help?"

Webb looked at her. "Would you mind? It could take hours, but once I see them in black and white, I frequently notice something I've only registered subconsciously. If I can pinpoint it now, we *might* prevent another murder."

"You can use the corner table. I'll move the lamp over." Hannah lifted the vase of sweet-smelling stocks and put it on the mantel-shelf. Webb followed her across and slid into the bench seat. As soon as she put the paper in front of him, he

began to sketch the rapid, startlingly lifelike cartoons of which
Michael Romilly of the *Broadshire News* could never get
enough. Hannah, who'd not seen him in action before,
watched, marvelling, over his shoulder. The first quick strokes
were enough for her to recognize the Walker family and their
friends, the perceptive line given to mouth or eyes indicating an
acuteness of observation which married the training of both
artist and detective.

Within minutes the sheet was peopled with familiar faces:
Fay, dreamily cradling her doll; Melanie, sowing the seeds of
'murder,' Gavin, Neville, Ashley—lovely even in caricature—
Howard, hesitant and bespectacled, Dick Ridley, the Tenbys,
Eleanor. Enthralled, Hannah slid onto the bench beside him,
content to sit in silence and watch.

Time ticked by. The incisiveness of the first strokes slowed to
doodle as Webb filled in background, adding props. Arthur,
curious to know what absorbed them, leapt lightly onto the
table and settled down to watch.

The first sheet of paper was pushed aside and Webb embarked on another. Specific scenes this time, map-like in their
accuracy: the drawing-room with the open window, the body
sketchily in place; the terrace, by which the murderer might
have gained entrance; the woodshed, which, mercifully, she
herself had not seen.

Then, on another sheet, characters and places came together,
each where he or she had claimed to be at the time of first one
murder, then the other. She appeared herself here, lying by the
pool, and it was uncanny to realize that for the moment this
was how David saw her, cartoon character rather than real
woman. Neville was shown with a suitcase, indicating his business trip, Lydia at her French class, Dick Ridley collapsed at
the bottom of the hill.

After a while, Hannah made coffee, silently placing a mug
beside Webb. He grunted acknowledgement, reached for it, and
drank, but his eyes never left the paper.

There followed a long, silent time in which no more drawing

took place. Webb stared broodingly at first one sheet, then another, comparing and contrasting the known facts with impressions his subconscious had interpreted.

Hannah retired to a more comfortable position on the sofa. Pirate returned from his nightly prowl, leaping onto a chair to join Oswald and jostling for dominant position. Arthur remained unmoving on the table, squinting sleepily.

It was after one o'clock, and Hannah's head was drooping over her book, when Webb suddenly sighed and stretched himself.

"That'll do," he said. Then, "Good Lord, is that the time? Love, I'm sorry! You should have told me!"

"I wouldn't have interrupted for the world."

"I doubt if they have a night porter at the Horse and Groom."

She smiled sleepily. "Surely everyone knows a conscientious detective works throughout the night?"

He grinned. "At one thing or another. May I stay?"

"I thought you'd never ask." She stood as he came across and moved into his arms, resting against him. "Was the marathon worthwhile? Anything new strike you?"

"One or two question-marks which will have to be clarified."

"But you haven't unmasked the killer?"

"Let's just say I have an idea."

She leant back, looking curiously up into his face. "Who? Do tell me."

He smiled and shook his head. "I might be on the wrong track, but it's been a worthwhile exercise; it almost always is. Thanks for putting up with it."

Jackson was already at the church hall when Webb arrived the next morning.

"Well, Ken, how were things at the Old Rectory last night?"

"I think negative's the word, Guv. Fay'd come round but not said anything important. No one admitted knowing TG, and I think we can discount the divorce. It was five years ago, and both parties are happily remarried."

"Did you come across anything more in the diaries?"

Jackson grinned. "They make good reading, don't they? Reckon it's true, or was he romanticizing?"

Webb thought briefly of Ashley. "I'd say it's true, all right."

"Well, there was nothing to help us in the one I went through. I passed the other to Sally; she might be luckier. We've had a break this morning though: the SOCO's have found a gardening apron and gloves pushed into the compost heap. They're splashed with what looks like blood."

"So that's why a change of clothes wasn't necessary. Let's get over there."

They walked together across the road. The day was overcast and the atmosphere clammy. Webb ran a finger round the collar of his shirt, looking up at the sky. "Hope it doesn't rain till they've got all they can out of the scene."

Access to the right-hand end of the garden was still under guard. The constable touched his helmet to Webb. "Inspector Hodges is expecting you, sir. He—"

But Dick Hodges was already emerging from the trees. "Ah, Dave. You've heard our news?"

"Yes, well done."

"He must have stashed them immediately after. He'd time on his side; no one was likely to come down here, and it's fully screened from the house. Makes it pretty cold-blooded, though. Assuming that his victim was chopping logs, he'd have had to pass him to get to the shed for the gloves and apron. The family say they were kept there, and if you remember, the door was open."

"But they must have exchanged words. Robin couldn't have failed to see him. Or her."

"A row, you mean?"

"I doubt if they discussed the weather."

"OK, then, how about this: they had a row, Robin turned dismissively back to his logs, and Chummie nipped into the shed for the gloves. Then, as Robin turned to see what he was doing, he knocked him to the ground, the axe fell out of Robin's hand and Chummie picked it up and gave him the chop. Quite literally."

"Succinctly put. And since he gowned himself like a surgeon, there was a degree of premeditation. But how much? Did he intend to kill Robin when he went down there or only after their conversation?"

"Search me. Any idea who it could have been?"

"Any bloody one of them," Webb said disgustedly. "They were spread about all over the place." He paused. "Could a girl have done it, Dick?"

Hodges gave him a surprised glance. "If she was self-possessed enough to fit the scenario."

Which surely ruled out Fay? Melanie, then? She'd accused her grandmother of murder, but what had either of them against Robin? On the other hand, Fay had been talking to him just before his death. What about? It seemed imperative to find out.

"Any chance of prints from the inside of the gloves?" he asked Hodges.

"Don't worry, we'll do our best."

Webb nodded. "I'll be at the house if you want me."

Lydia said doubtfully, "Do you really have to question her? I don't want a relapse."

"We'll go gently, Mrs. Walker, but she'll still be cushioned to some extent by the sedative."

"Will it be all right if I stay?"

"Of course, as long as you let her answer for herself. Where is she?"

"In the conservatory. I'll send for some coffee; it will make it seem less formal."

As they were crossing the hall, Sally Pierce approached him. "Could I have a quick word, sir? It might be important."

Webb gestured Jackson to go ahead with Lydia. "Yes, Sally?"

"Sergeant Jackson gave me this notebook to read, and I've been flicking through it. I found something I think you should see."

Webb took the book from her, angling it in the dim hall to get the maximum light. "3rd November," he read. "I was dreaming of The Girl again last night. God, if only I could stop!"

He looked up, frowning. Sally was watching him eagerly. "I am right, aren't I, sir? It looks as though TG didn't stand for anyone's initials, but just for 'The Girl.' "

Webb whistled softly. "He couldn't even bring himself to use her initial. 'If my soul's damned, it will be because of her.' *Fay?*"

Sally's green eyes widened. "I hadn't got that far. *Could* it be? Could *he* have been the father of her child?"

"That, as they say, is the question. Where's Inspector Petrie?"

"Here, sir."

"I'd like you with us; you might be needed. Thanks, Sally, that was very well spotted."

He walked briskly through the dining-room and into the warm brightness of the conservatory. Even on this grey day, stored sunshine warmed the atmosphere. His mind was churning with half-grasped truths, recoiling from, though at the same time accepting, what now seemed to be the case. As for the questions he must ask, he dreaded Lydia's reaction as much as Fay's.

Fay herself was hunched on one of the chintz-cushioned chairs. She looked pale and red-eyed, but calm enough.

If she'd been through what he now suspected, how could she be other than what she was?

"Are you feeling better?" he began gently. She nodded. "Fay, what were you talking to Robin about on the terrace yesterday?"

"I asked why he'd let them take the baby."

Lydia made a sudden movement which Webb quelled with a gesture. The drug Pringle had given Fay seemed to have low-ered her inhibitions, and she was speaking more freely than usual. Webb was duly grateful.

"Did you want to keep it?"

"Of course I did."

"Then why didn't you tell your parents?"

"I thought Robin would stop them. Right up to the end, when I went into hospital, I was sure he'd come and save us."

Lydia, frowning and perplexed, still did not understand. "But why should he, darling?"

Fay met her mother's eyes with a limpid gaze. "Because," she said simply, "it was his baby too."

Lydia gasped, half rising to her feet, then sinking back, her horrified eyes on her daughter's calm face. "Fay, that's a wicked thing to say! You know quite well that Clive—"

"Please, Mrs. Walker," Webb interrupted. "I realize this is distressing for you, but we must get at the truth. Now, Fay; Robin did know about the baby?"

"Yes, I told him."

"And what did he say?"

For the first time, the girl showed signs of distress. "That he'd think of something. Then he went to London and stayed away three weeks. And while he was there, Melanie found out about the baby, and then everyone knew. I thought he'd come back and explain, but all he did was ring to tell Granny he was going to marry Eleanor."

Lydia whispered, "I can't believe this . . . it's sick."

Webb could only agree. Holding down his own anger and disgust, he said gently, "Did he ever frighten you?" God, there were experts to deal with this kind of thing. Unfortunately, he couldn't afford to wait for them. Murder was involved and could be again.

"I was frightened at first and I didn't like what he did, but he was always kind."

"Always?" Lydia said in a strangled voice. "You mean it wasn't just once? When did this start, for God's sake?"

"My first term at Ashbourne," Fay said promptly. "I was home with a cold, and you asked him to keep an eye on me."

"You were seven years old!"

"Yes. He explained it was a very special kind of loving, but it must be kept secret, because people wouldn't understand and would be jealous."

Lydia said softly, "My poor baby! Oh, my poor little girl!" She turned agitatedly to Webb. "When she was a baby, she was always trotting after Robin. I used to think he was very patient with her. God, if I'd known what was in store, I'd have strangled him with my bare hands."

Footsteps were approaching from the dining-room behind them, and the maid Phyllis, with an anxious look at their set faces, put the coffee tray down on the table. Lydia seemed not to notice her, so Webb murmured his thanks and she withdrew.

Nina poured the coffee and handed round the cups. Everyone took one automatically.

Lydia was lost in her private hell. "After we came here, Robin often used to work at home. If one of the children was off school for some reason and I had to go out, I'd ask him to look after her. Melanie never minded, but Fay used to cry. I thought she was just being spoilt, and made her stay with him. Oh my *God!*" She turned her wild face to Webb. "Was it my fault? Did I make it happen?"

"You mustn't think that," he answered quietly. "And anyway it's over now. She'll be given expert help, but she'll need all the support you can give her."

"I'm *glad* he's dead!" Lydia said in a low, vicious voice. "Glad, glad, glad!"

Webb glanced at the girl, but she seemed not to be listening, lost in her own dreams. He raised his voice slightly. "Fay, had you asked Robin before why he didn't help you?"

She shook her head. "The baby was dead; there was no point."

"Then why bring it up yesterday?"

Fay sipped her coffee. "Because we'd all been talking about babies—Granny not able to have any, and everything. Then I heard him shouting at Eleanor, and when he came round the corner onto the terrace, it seemed a good opportunity."

"And what did he say?"

"At first he stared at me as if he didn't know what I was talking about. Then he said, 'At least it wasn't incest after all. I suppose that's something.' "

Lydia began to weep softly into her handkerchief. Webb wondered dully how many more tears this family would shed.

"And that was all?"

"Yes. He went down the steps and walked across the lawn towards the trees."

Webb said carefully, "Did you go after him?"

Fay seemed unaware of the implications of the question. "There was no point," she said again.

"So where did you go?"

"To the dining-room. I just sat down and waited for everyone else."

Webb glanced over his shoulder at the dim room behind him. If she'd looked through the conservatory windows, she'd have seen the trees behind which the murder was committed. "Did you notice anyone else go in that direction?"

But Fay shook her head. "I had my back to the window."

Which, Webb told himself resignedly, was sod's law. Then, as he thought over what he'd heard, something clicked into place and he realized that one of the question-marks he'd mentioned to Hannah had been explained. There seemed to be motive and opportunity for this last murder, and the means was bloodily to hand. So what about the first one?

CHAPTER 14

Webb assembled his staff who were still at the house—Nina Petrie, Jackson, and Sally—in the library.

"I've an idea," he told them, "and I need to be alone to think it through. In the meantime, I want you to turn your attention back to the first murder and go over again *exactly* where everyone was at the time of death, which is now established as between three-thirty and three-fifty on Wednesday.

"Ken, you drive out to Dormers and check on those three, particularly young Gavin, who admitted being here immediately after the murder. You two women can divide this lot up. And there are some specific questions I want you to ask, if possible without giving them too much significance."

They listened intently as he outlined them. "We'll meet for a pub lunch at the Horse and Groom," he finished, "at twelve-thirty. I'll book the parlour so we can talk freely."

He got to his feet. "Before you take the car, Ken, I want some papers out of it. I'll walk over with you."

As they crossed the road, the church bells were ringing joyously from the restored tower, a familiar Sunday-morning sound far removed from bloody murder. Small groups of people were walking towards the church, being careful not to stare up the drive of the Old Rectory as they passed.

"It would be Sunday," Webb commented. "I need to make some phone calls, but they'll have to wait till morning." He extracted the drawings he'd made at Hannah's from the back seat of the car. "OK, Ken; see you at twelve-thirty."

Back on the pavement, he turned in the direction of the church. The paved road finished at its gate, but to the left a small track followed the line of the graveyard wall and, beyond it, continued up the hill. This Webb took, occasionally looking back as the ground rose to see the diminishing figures still walking up the church path. He was almost on a level with the tower now, but there was no one up there today. Incredible to remember it was only eight days since he'd leant over its parapet and seen flowery "murder" in the garden below—a portent, had he known it, of not one but two violent deaths.

The bells stopped abruptly, and in the sudden silence he heard the low murmurings of an English summer; the hum of a bee close at hand echoed by the distant buzz of a lawn mower, a cricket chirping to his right, and, far away across the village, the barking of a dog.

He turned to look back over Honeyford. Not such a clear view, on this cloudy day, as from the tower in the sunshine, but he'd little suspected then how well he'd come to know this place. Now, he could pick out the various buildings and the thread of the main road leading to Dormers.

His thoughts turned again to Ashley. She and the others would need all their courage if what he suspected proved true. In one short week, an apparently close and happy family had dissolved into chaos, and there was more to come.

They'd seemed so secure within their charmed circle. Those on whom the gods smiled—the beautiful people—the Six Proud Walkers.

Yet Eleanor, the outsider, had seen beneath the facade. "Riddled with complexes," she'd said.

The first visible crack had appeared with Fay's pregnancy. According to Melanie, Dorothy Walker's insistence on abortion was to protect the family name. Well, it was beyond protection now. Yet the rot had started much earlier, with Robin's corruption of the infant Fay, violating her body, warping her mind, even while he loathed himself for it. The outward picture of a loving, supportive unit had always been false, hiding as it did corrosion within.

Webb sighed and unfurled the sheets of paper he'd brought

with him. In the light of new knowledge, he studied the drawings he'd made of people and places and nodded his satisfaction. It was certainly possible. And since the same hand must
surely have struck twice, he must now feel his way through the
alibis to expose their weaknesses.

By the time the church bells again rang out, he was sure he had
the solution. The answers the others were obtaining should
confirm it. There was no sense of triumph though; too many
people had been hurt and would be again.

He got to his feet, brushed the grass from his trousers, and
set off down the hill, again to the accompaniment of the bells.
As he passed the church gate, people were gathered in small
groups, talking in low voices. He'd no doubt what they were
discussing.

The landlord of the Horse and Groom readily agreed to his
request for privacy. "You'll be undisturbed in here, Mr. Webb,"
he assured him, holding open the parlour door. "Will you have
something to drink now or wait for your colleagues?"

"I'll have a pint to put me on, thanks."

The room was small and bright, with quarry-tiled floor and a
large brick fireplace. No doubt log fires burned in the winter;
now the dark mouth of the grate was screened by a brass
jardinière filled with hollyhocks.

Webb walked to the window. It was at the side of the building and looked onto an enclosed yard where a small child
squatting on the ground played with coloured bricks. For several minutes he watched her as she placed one on top of another and, when the pile unfailingly collapsed, stoically began
again. And he was witness to the small miracle of learning that
led her at last to place the bricks more centrally, so that the
edifice grew.

No lover of small children, Webb nevertheless felt a surge of
protectiveness, hoping with a fervour that surprised him that
she would be spared the mutilation of spirit that had withered
Fay.

He smiled wryly and turned from the window. He always waxed philosophical at this stage in a case and was relieved when the return of the landlord with a brimming tankard ended his musings.

"Bad business, up at the Rectory," the man said, shaking his head. "Think you're on to the culprit, sir?"

"I hope so, Mr. Layton."

"Well, that's good news, I must say. Custom's been falling off a bit; folks are nervous out after dark, with a killer on the loose."

They're quite safe, Webb thought privately, as long as their name isn't Walker.

Voices in the passage outside made the man turn, and Nina and Sally appeared in the doorway. Over his shoulder, catching Webb's silent query, Nina gave a brief nod. Webb let out the breath he'd been unaware of holding.

"Right, landlord, drinks for the ladies, and perhaps you'd bring us a menu."

As the door closed behind him, Webb said, "We'll wait for Sergeant Jackson. He'll want to hear all the details."

Jackson arrived with the drinks, having added his own to the order. The menu was passed round, and they chose quickly, each of them now anxious to embark on the discussion.

Webb looked round at their faces, solemn, apprehensive, curious. "You start, Inspector."

"I didn't see Mr. Walker," Nina began. "He was on duty at morning service and hadn't come back by the time I left."

"On duty, the day after his brother's death?"

"His wife said he was glad of something to do. As you suggested, I asked her when the business trip was first mentioned, and she said earlier in the week. There'd been a complaint, and there was the chance of losing a big order if things weren't smoothed over. At breakfast on Wednesday, though the visit hadn't been finalized, he was expecting to go. He'd asked her to pack his overnight case, and he was wearing what she called his 'tycoon suit,' the one he always chose when he wanted to impress people."

Webb leant forward. "Go on."

"I asked her to describe it. She seemed surprised, but said it was dark grey, with a thin red line in the cloth."

"He wasn't wearing it when he returned to the factory," Webb said positively. "That suit was also grey, but plain flannel. I noticed it particularly, because I've a similar one myself."

Jackson whistled softly. After a moment, Nina continued, "I also asked, as you suggested, if he took an extra suit with him on business trips. She said no, just a clean shirt and underclothes."

"And you checked upstairs?"

"As soon as I had the description, I sent a note out to Sally as we'd arranged."

Webb turned to the WDC, who took up the story. "I was interviewing Melanie, sir, but when I got the note, I made an excuse and ran up to the bedroom. That suit's definitely not in his wardrobe."

"Did the others confirm he was wearing it on Wednesday?"

"Yes, both the girls referred to it as 'Daddy's tycoon suit.' I asked if they'd seen it since, and they said no, he only wore it if he had a meeting."

"So far, so good."

A tap on the door heralded a short-skirted waitress bearing a tray with their lunches. The orders were sorted out, and, with a curious glance at them, she went out again, leaving the door ajar. Sally walked across and closed it.

"Did you check back, Ken, what time he got to Stratford?"

"Yes, we slipped up there, Guv. He didn't arrive till after five."

Webb swore softly. "As simple as that! It was the lunchtime phone-call that threw me; I assumed he'd left straight afterwards. Damn it, it was a business appointment he was going to. But the routine check was made, and we've had that crucial piece of information all along. Why the devil did no one mention it?'"

They avoided each others' eyes.

"All right," he said, with a touch of humour, "you can say it! Because I never asked. My fault—I should have done. But what the hell was he doing, arriving for a business meeting as late as that?"

Jackson said, "I reckon it was more of a PR exercise. He had them to dinner at his hotel."

"So we come to the next big question. What time *did* he leave the factory?"

"Soon after three. I've just been to the Incident Room to check Bob's notes."

"And as we know ourselves, it takes some thirty-five minutes to drive from Ashmartin to Honeyford. Which," Webb continued deliberately, "if that's what he did, would get him to the Old Rectory within minutes of his mother returning home."

"And she blurted out the news of her illness and his adoption, and he lost his marbles?"

"That's my guess, provided we're on the right track—and I'm damn sure we are. He was always hot on family tradition; it would have knocked him sideways."

For a minute or two they ate in silence, their minds busy with this latest information. Then Sally asked curiously, "What put you on to him, sir?"

"Remember I said that with the second murder, the killer'd doubled his chances of being caught? I worked it back from Robin's death. You've not had your say yet, Sally, but I presume you asked Fay exactly where she and Robin were standing when they spoke about the baby?"

"Yes—near the open drawing-room windows."

"And," Webb said softly, "we know that was where Neville went when the family separated. Despite the impression he gave, he wasn't as shocked as the others to learn of the adoption, because, of course, he already knew. But hearing his mother's letter would have brought it all back, and like the classic murderer, he returned to the scene of the crime—as he admitted, for the first time since her death. Who knows what thoughts were going through his head? And just at that fraught moment, he overhears his young daughter ask his brother why he didn't save their baby. In his place, I'd probably have reacted as he did."

"So he watched Robin set off across the lawn, and followed him."

"Yes. Note he didn't make the mistake of claiming to be in the drawing-room all the time, which was just as well, because Howard and Gavin went in later for a drink. He said vaguely that he walked up and down the terrace, and there was no one to disprove it. It was a gamble that no one would look out of a window—Fay could easily have done—but they were all occupied with their own traumas and the gamble paid off."

"So what happens now?" Sally asked uneasily.

"We'll let them finish their Sunday lunch; then we'll go and pick him up. Better to have the interview at the nick rather than the house."

"It's silly, but I wish it wasn't him. I like him."

Webb nodded. "You'll find, Sal, that quite often the villains are more likable than the honest Joes. Neville Walker had a raw deal. The tragedy was that he couldn't cope with it. I keep remembering what he said when we last interviewed him: 'I had so much, and now I have nothing.' He really believes that, and he just couldn't take it."

They lingered over their meal and ordered coffee to follow, so it was two-fifteen by the time they left the pub.

"No need for you to hang about, Sally," Webb told her. "Write up the interviews; then you can go home."

"Thank you, sir."

Webb wished he could too. He wasn't looking forward to the afternoon.

At the Old Rectory, they were met with the information that Neville was at the church.

"Again?" Webb exclaimed. "I thought he was on duty this morning?"

"Yes, but there's a christening and the other church warden's on holiday."

"What time will he be back, then?"

Melanie shrugged. "About half-past three, I suppose."

There was nothing for it but to settle down and wait. They went over to the church hall and passed the time by bringing their diaries up to date. Jackson was keeping a weather eye on the church path. At three-fifteen, he reported that people were starting to come out of church. With a heavy heart, Webb went out into the warm afternoon, Nina and Jackson behind him.

At the church gate they stopped and waited while the family photographs were taken. The baby had started to cry, and the young mother was frantically jigging it up and down in her arms in an attempt to soothe it. Jackson, father of four, reckoned it was more likely to make it sick.

Eventually, the party made its way down the path to the waiting cars. There were two sets of grandparents and quite a large group of friends and relatives. As the last of them came through the gate, the detectives moved inside. The vicar was coming down the path towards them.

"Are you looking for me, Mr. Webb?"

"No, sir. Is Mr. Walker still inside?"

"Yes, he's locking up. He'll be out in a minute."

They had just reached the porch when the heavy door opened and they found themselves face to face with their quarry. There was an instant's frozen surprise. Then, before they realized what was happening, Walker reached forward, grabbed Nina by the arm, and pulled her inside. To their horror, Webb and Jackson heard the scraping sound of bolts being drawn. Webb hammered on the door.

"Mr. Walker, open up at once! I must warn you that assaulting a police officer is an offence!" Even to himself, his words sounded hollow when addressed to a murderer. Through the thick wood, they heard Neville Walker's reply.

"And I warn *you*, Chief Inspector, that if you attempt to force entry, this young lady will be killed. I've nothing to lose, and I took the precaution of bringing a sharp kitchen knife with me."

"O God, Guv," Jackson said shakily, "what do we do now?"

"Go after the vicar. Ask him if he has keys to the other doors."

"But you heard what—"

"*Go*, Ken. And get Walker's wife. She might be able to talk some sense into him. I'll keep talking through the door and see if I can calm him down."

Inside the church, however, Neville had led Nina away from the door and sat her down in a pew off the centre aisle. He seated himself in the one in front, slewed round to face her, with the knife he had mentioned resting on the back of the pew.

"Sorry about the histrionics," he said calmly, "but I had to establish that I have the upper hand."

Nina's voice was equally calm. "It would be much more sensible to go out quietly. You haven't really got a chance, you know." She eyed the lethal point of the knife, and he followed her gaze.

"I assure you I'll use it if I have to, but please don't make me. They can't get in, by the way, so don't pin your hopes on that. All three doors are bolted and not easy to break down, even if they're prepared to risk your life by trying."

The smell of polish tickled her nostrils, overlaid by the faint perfume of flowers. On the gleaming pillars, black numbers on white indicated the hymns sung that morning. Nina wondered which they'd been. It all seemed so peaceful. Impossible to believe she was locked in here with a murderer.

She shuddered as the thought took root. What was the DCI doing? Would he manage to rescue her? How should she deal with this unstable man in front of her? Despite his calm voice, there was panic in his eyes. She said the first thing that came into her head.

"Mr. Walker, I'm so dreadfully sorry."

She saw his uncertainty, suspecting a trick. "For what?"

"For everything that's happened. Your world just fell apart, didn't it?"

"I'd so much," he said, paraphrasing Webb's words over lunch, "but it was built on a lie. All of it."

"Not all. Your mother loved you as if you were her own."

"No!" he said harshly.

"How did it happen?" She kept her voice quiet, mildly interested. Surely it would be a relief, now, to talk about it?

There was a long silence, in which she was able to hear even the faint ticking of her watch. Well, it had been worth a try. But then his voice came.

"I was about to leave for Stratford. I'd a difficult meeting ahead, and though I'd planned my approach, there were a couple of points I needed to clear with my mother. She'd a very sound business sense, you know. I buzzed her office, but Eunice said she'd gone home at lunchtime. If I'd known that, I could have spoken to her when I phoned Lydia. I rang again, but there was no reply. I didn't know about her appointment, so I thought she might be in the garden, and decided to call in on my way."

"And she'd just got back from the doctor's?" Nina prompted.

His eyes clouded, remembering. "She looked ghastly. For the first time, I saw her not as my mother but as an old woman. And before I could say anything, she started pouring out those terrible things, the words falling over each other in her haste to get them said. About the disease which was killing her, and as if that wasn't enough, the fact that it was hereditary. And while I was still reeling from that, she came out with the brain-numbing statement that I mustn't worry, because the three of us weren't her children anyway.

"Even then she went rushing on without pausing for breath,

and I was shouting at her to stop, to say it was all lies. Yet I knew somehow that it wasn't.

"I grabbed the poker just to threaten her, make her shut up, but the words still streamed out of her like some obscene discharge, poisoning the air. And then I was hitting her, over and over in a monotonous kind of rhythm. She went down at the first stroke, but by then I was incapable of stopping."

Nina said from a dry mouth, "And then?"

He smiled, a twisted rictus. "Then I realized I was covered in blood, and self-preservation took over. Suddenly completely calm, I stripped down to my underclothes and stuffed everything into a binbag. Then I went upstairs, had a good wash and changed into clean clothes. Incredibly, I'd only been in the house fifteen minutes."

"And no one saw you arrive or leave?"

"Honeyford's not a hive of activity on summer afternoons. But I'd forgotten Gavin was expected. It was sheer luck he didn't arrive while I was there."

"And you went on to your business meeting as if nothing had happened?"

"Yes. It's hard to explain, but the whole episode was blotted from my mind. It was such an enormity, so utterly inconceivable, that I convinced myself it couldn't have happened, it was a bad dream. That suspension lasted till I got back to the factory to find Webb waiting."

"And how did you feel then?"

"No compunction, if that's what you're expecting. I'd idolized that woman all my life, and she'd deceived me. There wasn't a vestige of affection left. How could there have been? She'd even contrived to do away with my grandchild. Lydia and I would have kept the baby, but she insisted on abortion. What *right* had she? Tell me that?"

"And your brother?" Nina asked after a moment. In the pause, her ears had been straining for any sounds outside the door, but she hadn't detected any. They'd be doing *something* though. Please make them quick; she wasn't sure how long she could keep him talking.

"Robin," Neville said, "was a filthy pervert, but he wasn't my brother."

"That made a difference?"

"Naturally. If he had been, I'd have flogged him and had him sent abroad. We have a factory in France, you know. I'd hardly have killed my *own* mother and brother. These people weren't related to me."

To which mad logic Nina could find no answer. He gave a brief laugh. "Here endeth my confession. We're in the right place, aren't we? I've bared my soul to you, and I don't even know your name."

"Detective Insp—"

"First name."

"Nina."

"Well, Nina," he began, and broke off as an odd sound came from behind the door. His hand tightened on the knife, and Nina braced herself, her heart fluttering in her throat. Blurred and distorted as though through a loud hailer, Lydia's voice reached them.

"Neville? Can you hear me?"

He sat immobile, his glazed eyes on the door. It took his wife's voice, so much a part of normal, everyday life, to bring home to him the truth of his position, barricaded in the church with a police officer held hostage. He, Neville Walker, church warden. And double murderer. He gave an odd, choked sound.

"Neville dear, please come out, and bring Mrs. Petrie with you. It'll be all right. I'm here."

Neville glanced back at Nina. "What am I likely to get?"

"You'll be examined by a psychiatrist, and if—"

"—if he thinks I'm mad, I'll spend my life in a padded cell rather than an ordinary one? Not much to look forward to, is it? How could they think it was merciful to abolish the death penalty? It's far preferable to life imprisonment."

"It very seldom *is* life," Nina said gently.

"You mean it might be only fifteen years? I'd still prefer to die." He got up slowly. "Anyway, that's what it says in the Good Book. An eye for an eye. Even more, surely, a life for a life. And I took two."

He stood looking down at her. Then he gave a deep sigh. "All right," he said, "you can let them in."

Hardly believing she was safe, Nina ran to the door, dragged back the bolts, and pulled it open. Webb caught hold of her.

"Nina!" Even in the panic of the moment, she registered that first use of her Christian name. She was accepted at last—one of the team. "Are you all right?"

"Yes, he—" Glancing back over her shoulder, she realized Neville was no longer in sight. "Where—" she began in bewilderment, but Webb was quicker.

"Get round to the tower!" he shouted over his shoulder. "Hold your jackets out—anything to break his fall!" Pushing past her, he dashed round the corner to the twisting staircase he'd climbed with Hannah the day it all began. As he hurtled round and round, he could hear other steps running above him. "Walker!" he called, his voice echoing against the stone walls. "Wait! For God's sake! At least let's talk about it!"

There was no reply. And when, seconds later, he reached the parapet, no one else was there.

"What'll happen to them now?" Hannah asked. It was the next evening, and they were on the patio overlooking the cottage garden.

"They'll survive," Webb said. "If they weren't a 'proper' family before, they certainly are now, and they'll stick together. My guess is Howard'll come into his own, which will please his wife. Up to now, he's been overshadowed by Neville's authority and Robin's glamour."

"But Lydia and the girls?"

"It'll take time, but Howard and Ashley will look after them. At least Fay has a chance, now everything's in the open.

If this last week hadn't happened, she might have ended up in a mental home."

"What I can't forgive," Hannah said, "is Neville allowing her to find Robin."

"He did ask Melanie."

"Even so—his own daughters! Why didn't he go himself?"

"Perhaps he couldn't face it. Or perhaps, in some twisted way, it was to punish them—Melanie for the flowers and her opposition to the abortion, and Fay for submitting to Robin and making it necessary for Neville to kill him. By that stage, you know, he wasn't entirely sane."

They were silent for a minute or two. Then Webb said, "Will you stay here for the rest of the month?"

"I'll have to. I can't take the cats back to the flat."

"You could be a great help to them, particularly Fay. Someone apart from the family but who knows the whole story."

"I'll do what I can."

"Thank you." He put an arm round her shoulders and drew her against him.

"Do *you* believe in Macbeth prophecies?" Hannah asked.

He gave her a little shake. "I do not," he said emphatically. "Nor in Father Christmas, the Tooth Fairy, or the Easter Bunny!"

"But seriously, David, *could* it have influenced him, seeing the word spelt out in scarlet like that?"

"Sweetheart, we spend our lives surrounded by influences of varying kinds. How we respond to them is what makes us different from each other."

"The fault lying not in our stars but in ourselves?"

"Something like that."

She sighed. "I suppose you're right." Then she smiled and reached up to kiss his cheek. "In that case, I might as well get supper."

ABOUT THE AUTHOR

Anthea Fraser, who lives in England, has published numerous novels both here and abroad; her work has been translated into seven languages. *Six Proud Walkers* is her fifth novel for the Crime Club.